NOTHING TO CROAK ABOUT

Silver Hollow
Paranormal Cozy Mystery Book 3

Leighann Dobbs
Traci Douglass

This is a work of fiction.

None of it is real. All names, places, and events are products of the author's imagination. Any resemblance to real names, places, or events are purely coincidental, and should not be construed as being real.

Chapter One

"Here we are," Issy Quinn said as she pulled her rusted-out old brown pickup truck up to the side of the dirt road on the outskirts of tiny Silver Hollow, New Hampshire, then glanced at her two cousins on the bench seat next to her.

"So sad," Raine said, undoing her seat belt then climbing out the passenger side door.

"Yes." Ember followed her two cousins out of the vehicle. "Very sad."

Issy walked around her vehicle, affectionately known as Brown Betty, to open the tailgate. "Poor Adele."

An old friend of their parents', Adele Brundage and her son, Scott, had lived in this run-down cottage in the woods surrounding town for as long as Issy could remember. Scott had been in Raine's class at school, and while he and the Quinns had not been the closest of friends, they were on friendly terms just the same.

His sudden death the week prior hit much too close to home.

Ember reached into the bed of the truck and pulled out a basket filled with chocolates from her shop, Divine Cravings, and a few gift certificates from Gray's hair salon, Sheer Magic. As the fourth Quinn cousin, he'd wanted to come with them today but couldn't due to his busy schedule.

"Maybe we should've taken donations or something." Issy frowned, gazing around the neglected property. Early autumn had settled over Silver Hollow, and while the daytime temperatures were still warm enough, the nighttime temps had grown chillier. There were even a few scattered trees whose leaves were starting to turn.

As the cousins started down the long drive toward Adele's home, their footsteps crunched on the thick bed of fallen needles from the fir trees surrounding them. The sharp scent of pine spiced the air, and the long shadows cast by the towering trees gave the whole area a slightly sad, depressed appearance.

Issy peered through the woods and noted that Louella Drummond's house wasn't far, maybe a quarter mile or so away. She tried not to think about Louella's place much these days, not just because Louella's murder had jarred the tiny, tight-knit paranormal community of Silver Hollow and brought them all sorts of unwanted attention. No. It was mainly due to a now-permanent resident of the area by the name of Dex Nolan who worked as an agent for the largest law enforcement group in the paranormal community—the FBPI, or the Federal Bureau of Paranormal Investigations. A branch of the regular FBI, they handled all the spooky things that went bump in the night, and were strictly top-secret in the human world. They weren't exactly welcome among paranormals either, considering they had a nasty reputation for carting any unfortunate paranormal they might take into custody to their also top-secret Area 59 compound where all sorts of rumored nefarious torture and testing practices took place.

She shuddered at the thought of herself or one of her beloved being whisked away to such a horrible place. All because they were witches. So unfair. Issy narrowed her gaze on a copse of trees far in the distance. If she wasn't mistaken, that was where Dex had found her the day she'd come out to Louella's cabin to do some investigating of her own into the murder case. That was where they'd talked a bit, gotten to know each other a bit better, shared their first kiss...

Her breath caught, and a prickle of heat climbed from beneath the scoop neck of her long-sleeved green T-shirt. Kissing Dex had been beyond nice, sure, but it could never go anywhere. They were too different—she was a paranormal. He was a man who'd dedicated his career to bringing in people like her. Issy sighed and hurried to catch up with her cousins.

"Why don't you just call him already?" Raine jostled against Issy as she adjusted her hold on one of two large blooming lily plants she'd brought for Adele. Raine's local landscaping business, Green Goddess Landscape and Florist, thrived because of her special gifts with plants. All she had to do was talk to them, show them a bit of special attention, and they grew year round, despite the weather. "You know you want to see Dex again."

Issy thought about playing dumb, but there didn't seem to be much point. She tried to brush the comment off instead. "I don't know what you're talking about."

"Oh, come on." Ember nudged Issy's arm with her elbow. The afternoon sunshine glinted off Ember's auburn-red curls and sparkled in her emerald eyes. Wearing one of her trademark blue gingham sundresses, she looked like a fairy-tale princess come to life. "I can tell by your dreamy expression that you're thinking about him. Not that I can blame you. Dex is a hunk, no way around it. Too bad he works for the enemy, since there was definitely something happening between the two of you that night at Enid's."

The last thing Issy needed to think about right now was that disastrous evening at Enid Pettywood's last month. That had been a most unfortunate night, when a demon had poisoned Ember and injured Issy as she'd tried to save Dex's life. And poor Raine... well, Issy was afraid Raine might never be the same after that incident. To distract herself, she grabbed one of Raine's lily plants and hoisted the heavy thing on her hip. "It doesn't matter what happened between us. Dex saw me use magic to exorcise the demon. He hasn't spoken to me since. I'm lucky he hasn't hauled me in for questioning. It's best if we just forget about it, okay?"

The three women headed up a narrower pathway toward the front door of the cottage. A few signs clung to the trunks of the trees here, dangling at odd angles. "Fortunes Told, Fee Charged," one proclaimed with a red arrow pointing toward the Brundage home. Below it was posted another sign, "No refunds."

Adele's magical specialty was prophecy, and she was well-known in town for having the largest collection of scrying balls in the Tri-State area. Given how many people sought out Adele's talents, Issy could see how the no-refund policy was probably a necessity. Fortunes weren't always pleasant, and some people didn't like what they heard. Many had left disgruntled when their fortunes weren't to their liking.

As if sensing Issy's thoughts, Raine gave a defeated sigh. "Too bad Adele hadn't been able to see into her son's future and prevent the tragedy."

Ever since the incident with the demon, Raine hadn't been her usual snarky, upbeat self. None of what had happened had been her cousin's fault, of course, but Raine had seemed more aloof and less trusting ever since. Side effects from battling the demon, perhaps? Whatever it was, Issy hoped the changes were only temporary. "Especially after poor Scott was on trial and in prison with no bail for a crime he didn't commit."

"You mean the murder of that girl from Lowell, Massachusetts? That was awful." Ember stopped to pick up a few stray pinecones. "Then living on the streets after he got paroled. That poor, poor man."

Poor man was right. Poor Adele too. Issy shook her head. The whole thing was a travesty.

Over the past ten years, Adele had spent every cent she had on lawyer fees to defend her son after he'd been accused of murdering a girl on a college spring break trip to Costa Rica. In the end, there'd never been enough evidence to convict him, but that didn't stop law enforcement from returning every few months with some new theory. They'd arrest poor Scott again, hold him for twenty-four hours, then release him back onto the streets when they didn't have enough to hold him. Eventually, the constant accusations took their toll. Scott couldn't get work and turned to drugs to numb his pain. Addicted and disillusioned, he'd moved out of Adele's home and joined the small homeless population living on the fringes of Silver Hollow.

Still, Adele had fought tirelessly to prove his innocence, despite the financial burden. She'd managed to earn enough money from her fortune-telling to keep her head above water, but just barely—as evidenced by the dilapidated state of her home.

"Seems weird not to have the kitties with me today," Ember said, running her hand over the top of her basket where her familiars Bellatrix and Endora usually rode. Issy had left her own familiar, an orange Pomeranian named Bella, back at her store, Enchanted Pets, in the care of her trusted assistant. Bella was becoming better and better at her duties as Issy's familiar each day, and she didn't want to risk hampering the tiny Pom's progress by bringing her to such a somber location. Mortimer, Raine's Venus flytrap familiar, had stayed home at her greenhouse as well.

"Ready?" Issy asked, stepping onto the creaky wooden steps leading to Adele's front door. A slight breeze ruffled her corkscrew strawberry-blond curls. "We won't stay long. I just wanted to offer my condolences again and make sure Adele's doing okay."

"The funeral was nice." Raine fiddled with the strap of her green overalls and shifted her weight from one foot to the other on the rickety porch, making it squeak even more. "Did you see Troy Holland was there?"

Issy nodded. Holland was a local bigwig, president of the family's paper mill. "Len Childs too."

"Those two have always been joined at the hip." Raine patted her stick-straight copper hair secured with a bandana that exactly matched the color of her peridot-green eyes. "Hardly surprising old man Holland named Len VP of the mill before he died. The Hollands had all but adopted Len by that point." Raine sighed. "I remember those guys were something else in high school. Always playing practical jokes and trying to outdo each other with the ladies. Scott kept up with them too, once they all left for college, at least until…"

Raine's voice trailed off, and Issy placed an arm around her cousin's shoulders, giving her a reassuring squeeze.

"I heard Troy helped Adele and Scott financially, after the trial," Ember said.

"I heard that too." Issy gazed once more across the woods to the spot where she and Dex had kissed the first time. Melancholy squeezed her chest. She liked Dex, far more than was prudent given what had happened at Enid's, but it was time to stop moping about it and move on. Her girlish crush seemed so unimportant now when compared to everything Scott and Adele had gone through. Chances were high Dex wouldn't want anything to do with her anyway now, and she had to accept that.

"Seriously." Ember nudged Issy once more, giving her a gentle smile. "Call him. Communication works both ways, you know."

"I can't," Issy said. "He saw me use magic, and Luigi couldn't erase his memory this time. Now he knows I'm a witch, and human-witch relationships never work, especially with his line of work. There's no future for us. It's over." Which was too bad because prior to the showdown with the demon, Issy had gotten a feeling they were actually getting somewhere and that maybe things really could work out. Probably just wishful thinking.

Ember's smile faltered. "Well, much as I dislike the FBPI, Dex seems to be a decent person. After all, he's not turned any of us in. He likes you, Issy, and I know you like him. Don't throw that away by being stubborn. Besides, you two are soul-bonded now."

Soul-bonded. Issy squeezed her eyes shut. She'd saved Dex's life that night at Enid's, and according to legend, if a witch saved a human's life she was soul-bonded to that human forever. Unfortunately, the bond only went one way, meaning Dex would never have any idea of his bond to Issy, nor would he have any urge to obey it.

"That's just an old wives' tale." Issy sighed.

"Sometimes people aren't meant to have a happily ever after," Raine said, her tone dark as a thunderstorm. "Sometimes bad things happen to good people, people who don't deserve it, and you just have to deal with it." She shifted the huge Easter lily pot on her hip and rolled her eyes at Issy. "Stop being such a Pollyanna, Em."

"I'm not being a Pollyanna." Ember frowned at Raine. "Why are you so negative lately?"

"Who's a Pollyanna?" Brimstone trotted up onto the porch, his hellfire-orange eyes glowing from his pudgy, charcoal-gray face. He was the oldest and wisest familiar Issy had ever met, not that she'd tell him that. The feline's ego was big enough as it was. Brimstone gazed around at the three Quinn cousins then proceeded to take a seat and groom his front paws. "Typical. Seems I'm the only familiar brave enough to hang out with you girls."

"Hey," Ember said. "Endora and Bellatrix are coming along just fine."

"So is Bella." Issy hugged her plant pot tighter. "She's communicating with me telepathically now."

"How exciting," Brimstone said, his bland tone implying the exact opposite. "What about Morty? Does he have root rot or something?"

"No." Raine glared at the sarcastic cat. "Mortimer's catching some afternoon rays today. He looked so content I didn't have the heart to move him, that's all."

"Sure." Brimstone sounded completely unconvinced. "Well, are you ladies planning on actually going inside the house anytime soon?"

Issy gave him a side glance then stepped up to Adele's front door. Except when she raised her hand to knock, the door creaked open. She frowned and looked back at her cousins. "That's weird."

"I better check things out." Brimstone slipped past Issy's ankles and into the house.

"Brimstone," Issy hissed. "Get back here."

No answer.

She went ahead and knocked anyway to be polite, even though the door was now ajar. "Adele? It's Issy

Quinn. I've got Ember and Raine with me. We stopped by to check on you and see how you were holding up."

Nothing.

"I've got a bad feeling about this," Raine whispered.

"Me too," Ember agreed.

Inside, Brimstone hissed loud.

"Come on!" Issy rushed inside, her cousins close on her heels and her pulse thundering in her ears. The small house was eerily quiet. Too quiet. They quickly searched the living room then rushed down the short hall to check the two bedrooms.

Adele was nowhere to be found.

"Girls, get in here!" Brimstone yelled from the kitchen.

The Quinn cousins ran in to find the older lady sprawled on the scuffed linoleum floor, pale and unmoving. Issy pressed her trembling fingers to the side of Adele's neck and found a pulse, faint but present.

"Stop it!" Brimstone cried. A whirling ball of energy chased him all around the kitchen. From what Issy could tell, it was a failed protection spell spinning out of control. Had Adele been attacked and tried to protect herself?

"I'm calling 9-1-1." Raine pulled out her cell phone.

Ember knelt on the other side of Adele and gently patted her cheek. "Adele, sweetie. Wake up. Can you speak to us?"

Adele's eyes snapped open, and she gripped Issy's hand tight.

"What happened, Adele?" Issy asked.

"They hit me from behind," the older witch rasped. "Got me good too."

While Raine called for help, Issy carefully examined Adele's head. The hair near the back of her scalp was matted with blood. Given the small pool of crimson dried on the floor nearby, poor Adele must've been lying there injured for quite a while.

"Who did this to you?" Issy said, her voice quivering.

Adele's gray eyes clouded over, and she coughed, the sound congested and desperate. "I didn't see them. I'm not long for this world, Isolde." She tugged Issy closer, surprisingly strong for a woman of her age, her expression fierce. "I won't go quiet, though. I want vengeance!"

"I think it's a bit premature for that." Issy's heart twisted as Adele's pale face turned even paler. "Hold on, the ambulance is coming."

"It's too late," Adele rasped. Her eyes drilled into Issy's, holding her gaze like a magnet. Issy couldn't look away if she tried. "Someone did this to me, and I intend to make sure they pay. I curse a plague of toads on Silver Hollow until my killer is found!"

Before Issy could respond, Adele's body convulsed and her head fell back as her last breath wheezed out of her.

Chapter Two

"Police are on their way." Raine ended her call. "Oh no!"

Issy said a quick blessing over Adele's body then hung her head. "She's gone."

Ember sniffled. "Who would have done something like this?"

"No idea." Issy glanced over at Brimstone. "We need to neutralize that protection spell, though, before it drives our old friend crazy."

The whirling ball of energy zipped after the cat, gathering momentum and small objects in its wake—bobby pins, a skein of yarn, a pot holder.

Brimstone hissed, arching his back and batting at the thing. "Stop it!"

"Adele must've cast the spell after she was hit to protect herself," Ember said. "In her dazed state it didn't materialize correctly."

Sirens wailed in the distance.

Straightening, Issy pointed toward a cabinet hanging crookedly off the wall. "Get a bowl of water and some salt. Let's see if we can get rid of the spell before Owen and DeeDee arrive."

Once her cousins had done as she'd asked, Issy closed her eyes, took a deep breath, and clenched her fists tight before unfurling them at the whirling energy. "*Novisio!*"

The glowing ball dissolved, the items contained in the tiny maelstrom falling to the floor moments before Deputy Deidre Clawson raced into the room. DeeDee took in the scene then the three Quinn cousins, her expression suspicious. "What's going on here, ladies?"

Brimstone yawned and stretched, giving his front paws a few more licks before heading calmly for the door, as if he hadn't just been chased by the miscast energy ball. "Since you all have things under control, I'll just be going now."

He darted outside before anyone could stop him.

Silver Hollow Sheriff Owen Gleason charged inside, wearing one of his trademark Hawaiian shirts again, instead of his official uniform. He tipped the brim of his baseball hat to the Quinns. "Howdy, ladies. Mind telling me how you three managed to show up at another crime scene? You gals seem to be magnets for trouble these days."

Issy glanced toward the door again, half hoping Dex might walk in next. Even though she knew his real job was to investigate paranormal activity for the FBPI, she knew he sometimes used his FBI credentials as an excuse to get involved in Silver Hollow police activity.

She turned back to face the crime scene and found Ember watching her with a smile.

"What?" Issy asked.

"Nothing." Ember's knowing grin widened. "Looking to see if a certain agent is on the case?"

"No."

"Looks like the EMTs are too late," DeeDee said as an ambulance pulled up outside. She knelt beside Adele and felt for a pulse. "She's dead."

A loud croak issued through the open door as a stretcher was wheeled in and Ursula Lavoie, the medical examiner, followed in behind it. Issy was surprised to see Ursula out during the day. Being a vampire, she liked to spend the daylight hours sequestered in the underground morgue and rarely visited crime scenes. Today, she wore a black jacket with the biggest hood Issy had ever seen. Ursula pushed the hood back, revealing porcelain-white skin, jet-black hair, and delicate features. She nodded at Issy and her cousins, then bent down to inspect Adele.

DeeDee pulled the Quinns aside. "Is there anything I need to keep from Owen?"

Their sheriff was human and had no idea about the paranormal community living under his jurisdiction. Issy glanced over at Adele as the EMTs gently loaded her onto the gurney, then back at the deputy. DeeDee, a werewolf shifter, had made it her duty to keep Owen in the dark about all things paranormal. Ursula helped by neglecting to mention some of the more paranormal aspects of the various deaths. Not that they wanted paranormals to get away with murder, but the community just preferred to deal with them on their own.

"No," Issy said. "We just stopped by to make sure she was okay."

"See? We brought gifts and everything," Raine added, pointing toward the plants and chocolates sitting on Adele's counter.

"What about all this stuff on the floor?" DeeDee nudged a bobby pin with the toe of her shoe. "What's all this about?"

"We think Adele tried to cast a protection spell after she'd been injured," Ember explained, her tone low. "Because of her compromised state, the casting went awry and formed an energy ball that gathered all these things inside it, like a mini-tornado."

"Once I banished the spell, all the stuff fell out," Issy said.

The EMTs wheeled Adele's body from the room just as a second officer showed up. Issy hadn't seen the guy before, so he must've been new to the force. Given the recent rash of crime in the tiny village, it seemed the Silver Hollow Sheriff's Department was expanding.

Owen walked over and held out a bunch of evidence bags to DeeDee before snapping on a pair of latex gloves. "Ursula says Ms. Brundage died from blunt force trauma to the head. You and Officer Dunlop process the crime scene initially until the CSIs get here. Make sure you dust all these knickknacks for fingerprints." He hiked a thumb toward the shelves full of crystal balls in the living room then frowned at the items scattered on the kitchen floor by the energy ball. "This place is a mess. Going to be hard to tell what's part of the struggle and what's just clutter. I'll have a look around and see if I can find the murder weapon."

"Yes, sir," DeeDee called as Owen headed outside, then handed a pair of gloves and several evidence bags to her underling. "Start in the living room, Dunlop."

"Got it, Deputy Clawson." The guy all but saluted before taking off into the other room.

"We've got to be careful around Owen," DeeDee said, once the guy was out of earshot. "He's become way more dedicated ever since the Pettywood incident last month."

Raine met Issy's gaze then looked away fast.

"I found something!" Owen yelled. He walked in with a heavy tree limb about the size and shape of a baseball bat. Dried blood caked one end of it. "I'm guessing it came from her stash of walking sticks. There's a whole container of them by the front door."

Issy looked to where he was pointing, and sure enough, there were walking sticks and what looked like regular tree limbs in a metal stand. She must've missed those in her haste to get inside earlier.

"How are you guys doing?" Owen asked.

"I put Dunlop on the living room, sir," DeeDee said.

"Okay, then." Owen walked into the next room and stood, hands on hips, staring at the ransacked bookshelves lined with scrying balls. Issy gave DeeDee a what-do-we-do-now look. Owen wrinkled his nose. "Wasn't Adele some kind of fortune-teller?"

"Um, yes," Ember said before Issy could stop her. "She used her crystal balls to tell someone's future." Issy gave her a stare. "Oh. Well... at least that's what she said."

"Right." Owen nodded. "Yeah. I've heard folks around here talk. Some of them really believe all that crazy hocus-pocus too." He snorted. "I bet not all of them like what she told them either."

"I suspect that's true," Issy said.

"Hmm." Owen picked up one of the balls in his gloved hand. "These things valuable?"

"Not terribly," Issy said. For those without the gift of foresight, they were nothing but pretty glass objects. "A hunk of polished rock crystal maybe worth a few bucks."

"Not worth killing over then?" Owen held the scrying ball in front of his face so his image was distorted.

"Probably not." Issy met DeeDee's gaze. Maybe Adele's gift had gotten her murdered.

"Too bad about her son, Scott." Owen set the ball back on its stand then made a slow trek around the perimeter of the room. Everything in the place was shabby—from the secondhand furniture to the worn rug and the outdated TV. "And now Adele. Doesn't seem like this was a robbery. Doesn't look like she had much."

"So why kill her and ransack the place then?" Officer Dunlop asked as he bent to look inside a cabinet. He hiked his gloved thumb toward the bookcase. "Especially if those crystal balls aren't worth anything. From the looks of this place, that's the most valuable thing she had."

"Perhaps the murderer wasn't looking for something of monetary value." Owen brushed past Issy on his return to the kitchen. He stood over where Adele's body had been minutes earlier. Blood still stained the floor, and DeeDee had placed various markers to show where pieces of evidence had been found. "Adele might have been killed because she surprised her attacker. Though I'm not sure how they got in. There's no obvious signs of forced entry, but her door is old and the casings already marked up, so someone could have jimmied the lock and those marks would be indistinguishable from what's already there."

Ember opened her mouth, but Issy gripped her arm to keep her quiet. None of them had mentioned the door being open when they'd arrived, and it was probably best to keep that to themselves for now, until they knew exactly what they were dealing with here.

Owen continued. "I'd say Adele Brundage probably saw something in one of her visions of the future and someone else didn't like it. They mostly likely didn't want her to tell anyone else about it either. So they came here and silenced her for good."

Chapter Three

Dex Nolan sat on the back deck attached to his quaint little bungalow, sipping his beer while a trio of toads hopped across the lawn. Gordon, his pet bearded dragon, dug his tiny claws into Dex's shoulder, watching the toads with great interest. Little guy probably thought they'd make a tasty snack.

"Hey, buddy," Dex said, tugging gently on the leash around Gordon's neck to distract him. "Best find something else to eat. Those things will give you warts."

The lizard flicked his tongue out to graze Dex's cheek and raised his front paw, as if waving hello. Considering he'd never expected to have a pet, bachelor Dex had quickly become best pals with Gordon.

"How about some pizza, huh?" Dex laughed when Gordon cocked his head to the side as if he understood the question. "No to pizza, huh? You'd probably prefer a few juicy grasshoppers, eh? Or maybe some flies?"

Sirens raced by in the distance, and Dex frowned toward the far side of his yard, closest to the street.

"Wonder what's going on, buddy. Sounds like quite a ruckus."

He set his beer aside and stood. While spending a lazy afternoon around his new house was nice and allowed him to finally get some of those boxes unpacked from when he'd moved in a few months ago, sitting on the sidelines wasn't Dex's style. He preferred to be in the thick of things. It was why he'd taken this job in Silver Hollow, after all. Well, that and a certain feisty strawberry-blonde who'd been ignoring him for the past two months.

With a heavy sigh, Dex headed back inside and set Gordon on the perch in his vivarium. Honestly, he understood now why the FBPI would want an agent at this location full-time, given the strange occurrences around these parts, but that didn't help keep his mind off Issy Quinn or that weird night at Enid Pettywood's.

Or maybe he should say *miserable* night. He'd failed to protect Issy from whatever the heck that thing had been that attacked her, so he couldn't blame her for not wanting to talk to him. Honestly, he'd gotten lucky that he'd only suffered the silent treatment. The last time he'd failed to protect someone put in his charge, a child had died.

He walked into his kitchen and tossed his empty beer bottle into the recycle bin. And yeah, afterward, he'd done his duty and filled out all the Bureau's required reports, telling them lightning had been responsible for the damage to the Pettywood house, when deep down he knew what had happened in that house was not due to any electrical storm.

Before coming to Silver Hollow, he'd never been a believer in the paranormal. He had taken the job with the FBPI mainly to assuage his guilt over that kid dying, then later had decided to stay on to be closer to Issy. Now, though, after what he'd seen that night at Enid's—the glowing malevolence in Raine Quinn's eyes, the way the demon had shifted before his eyes from human to something dark and evil, the sparks and power that had flown from its fingertips and rendered him paralyzed and injured Issy in the process...

A shudder ran through him. Well, now that whole situation had made him seriously consider that there really might be forces greater than he could see at work here in Silver Hollow. That perhaps the paranormal and magic weren't silly old fairy tales after all.

Distracted, Dex headed toward his bedroom for a shower. Surprisingly, the thought of real ghosts and ghouls and things that went bump in the night didn't disturb him nearly as much as he thought it would.

Maybe his time in the FBPI hadn't been a total waste after all.

As he flipped on the shower and got out a towel from the linen closet by the door, he couldn't help but worry, though, about his sworn duty to bring in those he suspected of possessing these strange, magical powers. Issy and her cousins hadn't just been there during the incident at Enid's. They'd been active participants in all the events and seemed to be mixed up in the paranormal happenings in the community. Which meant eventually Issy's and Dex's purposes would cross.

Stepping under the steamy spray, his frown deepened. If it came down to it, could he arrest Issy or any of her cousins for suspected paranormal behavior? No, Dex didn't think he could. He'd met them, spent time with them, knew them all to be decent people.

Arresting them seemed wrong.

Dex soaped up and scrubbed down fast, then dried off and changed clothes, pulling on a fresh pair of jeans and a T-shirt, wanting to be comfortable on his day off. Then he padded back out to his kitchen to see what he might fix for dinner. Cooking for one was kind of a drag, but he did the best he could.

While he stared into his fridge, the conflict between his personal feelings and the duties of his job circled in his mind. Really, if he played his cards right, he wouldn't necessarily have to arrest anyone—as long as he didn't write his reports to show any paranormal involvement in the cases he investigated, no one would be the wiser. He'd be able to protect Issy and her cousins and all the other good people he'd met here in Silver Hollow.

Yep. Sounded like a plan.

Now all he needed was official clearance from his boss back at headquarters to work on every case that passed through the Silver Hollow Sheriff's Department.

Dex set aside the loaf of bread and packet of lunch meat he'd pulled from the fridge and picked up his cell phone from its charger instead. Hitting the speed dial button, he rested his hips against the edge of the counter and waited for his old partner and new boss, Stan, to answer.

"Stanley Judge, FBI."

Wincing at the guy's clipped tone, Dex forced a smile. When it came to apprehending suspected paranormals, good old Stan gave new meaning to the word gung-ho. "Hey, Stan. It's Dex."

"Dexter Nolan. How are you?" Stan's tone became less abrupt, if no less formal. He and Dex might've been partners, but they'd never really been close friends. "Tell me something's finally happening down there in Silver Hollow."

Used to thinking fast on his feet, Dex remembered what he'd heard while out on his deck. "I think maybe there is. Sirens raced by here about half an hour ago. Sounded like a couple squad cars and maybe an ambulance. I was hoping you could do me a favor and call Owen's office. If he's got a new case, then I'd like to be his coinvestigator." He took a deep breath. "In fact, considering what we're dealing with here in the area, it might be in our best interest for you to give him a blanket order to involve me in all of his cases from here on out. That way we won't miss an opportunity to capture any paranormal activity going on around here."

"Wow." Interest sparked in Stan's voice at last. "I like your initiative, Agent Nolan! Reminds me of myself when I first started out with the Bureau. If things are truly getting exciting, maybe I should come there for a while too. We could get the old team back together."

Crap. Not what Dex had in mind. "Oh, well. I might've gotten ahead of myself there a bit. Honestly, I don't know what's going on at this point. Only that I heard sirens. Could've been a jaywalker for all I know." He forced a laugh that sounded fake even to his own ears and prayed Stan would back off.

"Oh." Disappointment and annoyance zinged through Stan's tone. "In that case, I'm far too busy to make the trip over if there's nothing going on. I'll call the sheriff, and you get the scoop. Make sure you call me back, though, if it's anything paranormal. I'd love to haul a couple of those degenerates into Area 59 for questioning."

The mention of the Bureau's top-secret interrogation facility made Dex's stomach cramp. He'd never been there himself, but the rumors of the torture and heinous deeds performed on the poor prisoners there made Gitmo seem like a walk in the park. If Issy or her cousins ever ended up in the place…

He shook his head and glanced over at Gordon in his enclosure, his racing pulse quieting. Stan had given him the okay to work on Owen's cases. That was a step in the right direction. From there, Dex would find a way to keep Stan away from Silver Hollow and things would be good.

"Will do." Dex exhaled in relief. "Thanks, boss."

"No problem. Keep up the good work, Agent Nolan."

He hung up before Dex could respond.

Dex smiled, tossing his phone back on the counter, feeling better than he had in weeks.

Finally, he'd have a new case, something to keep him busy and involved. And hey. If he happened to run into a certain Issy Quinn while on the job, you'd hear no complaints from him.

Chapter Four

"Well, that took forever," Issy said as she climbed in behind the wheel of Brown Betty once more. The pickup sputtered a few times and belched out a stream of noxious exhaust then chugged to life as her cousins got in on the passenger side.

"I can't believe Owen pawned us off on that new deputy," Ember groused. "Poor DeeDee kept giving me apologetic looks from across the room."

"Yeah, that Dunlop's a little too Barney Fife for my tastes," Raine said.

Issy carefully backed down Adele's driveway and out onto the dirt road once more. "So what do we do now? We can't just let Owen handle things. DeeDee can only cover up the paranormal aspects for so long." She took a deep breath and stared out the windshield. "Isn't there someone else living on this road?"

"Yes. Mr. Crandall," Ember said. "Ornery old hermit, from what I recall. He lives in a tiny cabin near the entrance to this road."

"Great." Issy started slowly forward. "Maybe we should pay a visit to him while we're here."

Raine rolled her eyes again. "Sounds like a perfect end to a less-than-stellar morning."

They neared the end of the dirt road, where it intersected with the main highway leading into Silver Hollow. Issy squinted through the thick trees on either side of them. "Are you sure he still lives here? I don't see anything."

"As far as I know, he's not moved." Ember leaned forward to see past Issy.

"Over here." Raine pointed out the passenger side window toward a barely visible roof through the tree line. Issy parked on the berm then got out.

Ember wasn't kidding about the place being small. Whoever this Mr. Crandall was, his abode went way beyond the latest tiny-house movement. The three cousins traipsed through the thick foliage and halfway up a hill to the squat little cottage nestled between two huge oak trees. From the worn exterior, it looked like Mr. Crandall had built the place himself out of rough-sawn wood. One peeling brown shutter creaked ominously in the steady breeze, and the minuscule porch squeaked loudly when Issy set foot on it.

"Oh my!" Ember cried.

"What's wrong?" Issy turned fast, her pulse tripping.

"Toads!" Raine pointed to two of them skittering over the top of Em's cute white pumps.

"Come on." Issy linked arms with Ember and pulled her up onto the porch. Raine trailed after them. "Let's see if Mr. Crandall's home."

She knocked on his door then took a step back, forcing a polite smile.

No one answered.

"Huh." She tried again, but still nothing. "Well, maybe he's not here right now."

"Oh, he's home all right," Raine said, pointing toward an eyeball peering at them through the drapes of a nearby window. "Want me to wave at him?"

"We should probably just go," Ember said. "Mr. Crandall is notoriously tight-lipped, from the rumors I've heard at my shop. I'm not surprised he won't let us in."

"You could've mentioned that before we walked all the way up here." Issy stepped down off the porch, her cousins following. Guess they'd just have to find out what happened to Adele some other way.

"What do you want?" a gruff male voice yelled from behind them.

Issy whipped around and spotted a short older man with snow-white hair scowling at them through a small crack in his front door.

"Mr. Crandall?" Issy flashed her friendliest smile and started back toward the tiny home. "My name is Issy. My cousins and I were hoping to talk to you about—"

"We're here about Adele Brundage," Raine called to him.

"I know who you are. You're the Quinns. Knew your parents. Remember seeing you all as babies." The old man looked at each of them then back to Issy again, his brown gaze suspicious. "What do you want with Adele?"

Stepping cautiously back up onto the porch, Issy was half scared the older man would slam the door in her face. "I'm so sorry to be the bearer of bad news, Mr. Crandall, but Adele Brundage was murdered."

"The devil you say." Mr. Crandall eased open his front door a bit wider. He couldn't have stood more than five feet high, and his shoulders were permanently slumped with old age. "Poor, poor Adele. I knew something wasn't right when all those police cars came racing up earlier. And then that ambulance. Terrible, terrible thing." He shook his head and frowned. "Adele was a nice lady. Didn't deserve the lot she got."

He started to go back inside and ease the door shut behind him, but Issy stepped forward and stuck her foot into the jamb to keep him from closing it all the way. "I'm sorry to bother you again, Mr. Crandall, but we were wondering if you might've seen anything strange going on at Adele's place recently?"

"Strange?" He glanced back at her over his shoulder. "No. I don't hear too good, and most of the time I just keep to myself and mind my own business, like most people should." His implicit tone wasn't lost on Issy. "Besides, with that fortune-telling business of hers, there was always a lot of cars and people coming and going."

"You don't remember seeing anything odd or maybe someone lurking around her home?"

"I really don't want to get involved," he said, starting to close the door again.

"Wait!" Ember raced up beside Issy. "I'm pretty sure I have an extra batch of that penuche fudge you love so much back at my shop, Mr. Crandall."

The door opened slightly wider again, and Mr. Crandall's expression brightened. "Oh, penuche fudge. I've not had that in a coon's age."

Ember smiled. "Well, then, I might just remember to bring you some. Memory is a tricky thing, though, like you said. Sometimes you have to think hard to remember."

Mr. Crandall narrowed his gaze. "I see. Yes, you're right. Now that I think about it, I did see something peculiar over at Adele's place. Not last night, wasn't nobody there then near as I could tell. Course I can't see much from here. Trees are too thick. But when there's a ruckus I look out, and yesterday afternoon I saw Jerry Blaisdale come peeling down the road in that red Honda Civic of his. That boy was hell-bent for leather, I'm telling you."

"About what time was that, Mr. Crandall?" Issy asked.

"Early afternoon. About two or so, I'd say."

"And you're sure he was at Adele Brundage's?" Raine asked.

Mr. Crandall gave her an annoyed look. "Where else would he be going, missy? Ain't nobody else live out this way except me and her."

With that he shuffled back inside, turning to face Ember as he grasped the side of the door. "Don't you forget my fudge now, you hear?"

Then he slammed the door shut in their faces.

"Okay, then." Issy blinked at the wooden door. "Well, at least we got a bit of new information."

"Yes." Ember linked arms with them, and the three Quinn cousins stepped down off the porch together, heading back through the woods to Brown Betty. "And all it cost us was a pound of fudge."

"I wonder when Adele was actually attacked. Couldn't have been that long ago. Certainly not yesterday afternoon when Jerry sped by." Raine held the door of the truck open for Ember. "Crandall likely wouldn't have noticed any other cars driving by in the middle of the night."

"She might've been lying in the kitchen for a while, but the blood around her head was still sticky," Ember said.

"True." Issy fastened her seat belt then started the engine. "But why would Jerry Blaisdale want to hurt Adele?"

"Not sure. He *has* been acting strange lately, though," Ember said, straightening the skirt of her sundress. "One of my customers told me the other day Jerry's emotions have been getting the better of him, and he's been casting spells by mistake."

"Really?" Issy waited for traffic to pass on the highway then turned out and headed back toward Silver Hollow. "Do you think maybe Adele foretold his problems with her scrying ball and he didn't want to risk her telling anyone?"

"Or maybe he cast an illegal spell," Raine said. "If Adele foresaw it, then she'd be honor bound to report it to Luigi, and he'd have to bring it up to The Committee for prosecution."

The Committee was the regional governing body for all the local covens and paranormal activity. They weren't nearly as bad as the FBPI when it came to punishments, but they could still make a paranormal's life miserable if necessary.

As Issy passed the sign welcoming them to Silver Hollow, a black Cadillac passed them on the two-lane highway. Issy glanced into her rearview mirror in time to see the car turn off down Adele's dirt road. "Huh. Why would you think a fancy car like that would go to see Adele?" she asked.

"Could be one of her clients who doesn't know she's dead," Ember said.

"Maybe." Issy checked both ways then made a U-turn and headed back toward Adele's. She slowed as they passed the entrance to the dirt road and spotted Troy Holland and Len Childs getting out of the Cadillac.

"What are they doing here?" Raine asked, crowding Ember to see out Issy's window. "I can't imagine they'd have much use for Adele Brundage or her talents now."

"Let's find out." Issy turned back down the dirt road. Ahead, tall, blond, handsome Troy straightened his preppy blazer then said something to Len. Len— thinner and shorter than Troy, with glasses and pockmarked skin—laughed and slapped Troy on the back. Even back in school, Troy had always seemed like the leader of the two.

Looked like nothing had changed.

As she pulled to a stop behind Troy's Cadillac, a fat toad hopped in front of her car. Adele's curse ran through Issy's mind once more.

A plague of toads on Silver Hollow until my killer is found...

The two men stood just to the side of the road, staring at all the squad cars clogging Adele's dirt driveway.

"What's going on here?" Troy asked as Issy and her cousins approached.

"We came by early and found Adele dead inside her house," Raine said, standing slightly back from the group with her arms crossed.

"She's dead?" Len asked, the color draining from his cheeks.

"Afraid so," Ember said. "She was actually still alive when we found her, but passed away shortly afterward."

"How awful." Troy seemed genuinely sad. "Did she say anything about what happened? Why would someone want to kill her?"

"No. Not a word." Issy watched the two men carefully. "The police are investigating now. She was struck from behind in the back of the head, so she didn't see her attacker."

A large, golden-eyed toad glared at Issy from the side of the road, urging her on.

"What are you guys doing here?" Issy asked.

Len looked from Issy to Troy then back again. "We stopped by to see how she was getting along too. Same as you. We hadn't seen her since Scott's funeral."

"I didn't think you guys hung out together anymore," Raine said, her gaze narrowed.

"We didn't really hang out, not since Scott's addiction problem got out of hand. Then the homelessness." Troy shook his head. "But I still kept in contact, and every so often I tried to reach out to him and offer my help, but Scott refused to change his ways."

"Do you know of anyone else who might've wanted to hurt Adele?" Ember asked.

"No, not really. Everyone liked Adele," Troy said.

"Scott hung out with some pretty unsavory characters, though," Len added. "Maybe she met one of them at Scott's funeral and they thought she got some kind of life insurance settlement after his death. Drug addicts will break in and steal just about anything." Len frowned. "You know, come to think of it, I do remember seeing one of the homeless arguing with Adele after the services."

"That's right," Troy said. "There were some problems at the wake."

"What problems?" Issy asked.

"Apparently one of those homeless people caused a ruckus after the wake," Troy said.

"About what?" Issy asked.

Troy shrugged. "Who knows. They can be unstable and get agitated easily."

"You said problems. What else happened?" Raine asked.

"That guy. Used to work security at the mill for Dad. That one that was a camera buff." Troy glanced at Len as if expecting him to refresh his memory on who it was.

"Jerry Blaisdale?" Raine offered.

"Yes!" Troy smiled. "He pulled Adele aside, and it looked like they were arguing."

"What about?" Issy scrunched her nose. Jerry might've been not quite himself lately, but she couldn't imagine the guy confronting someone like that at a funeral.

"Don't know." Troy shook his head. "I wasn't close enough to hear, but the discussion looked very animated. It was before the wake started. Len and I helped Adele get set up. I didn't try to eavesdrop or anything. I did notice she was upset, though, when she came back into the room, but I didn't want to pry." He gave an angry snort. "Can you imagine having the gall to argue with a woman at her own son's wake? Who would do that?"

Chapter Five

Later that night, all four Quinn cousins convened around their usual gathering spot—the fire pit behind Issy's house. The autumn air had turned cooler this evening. Add in a slight breeze blowing off the lake in the distance and it forced them all to bundle up. It didn't stop them from eating, though, and they had their usual snacks of veggies with dip, chocolate bark from Divine Cravings, popcorn, and s'mores toasted over the fire around which they all sat.

Despite the chill, toads croaked louder than usual in the night.

"Bella's doing so well with her lessons," Issy said, kissing her little Pomeranian familiar on the top of her furry head. "I told Brimstone earlier she's communicating with me telepathically now. Some of her messages are still gibberish, but they get clearer every day."

"That's great!" Ember said, pulling her two feline familiars—Endora and Bellatrix—from their basket. One kitten pure black, the other pure white snuggled into the fleece blanket spread across her lap. "The girls are getting more comfortable talking to me telepathically too, though we've still got a way to go."

Brimstone snorted from his spot at the end of one of the logs surrounding the fire pit. "Gee, maybe one day they'll actually earn the title of familiar."

"Bella doesn't have to earn anything," Issy said, giving Brimstone a look before holding up the tiny Pom and kissing her on the nose. "You're mommy's perfect little familiar, aren't you?"

The large charcoal-colored cat rolled his eyes and resumed his grooming.

"Morty looks good," Issy said to Raine while settling Bella on her lap again. "And he's got a guest."

Raine frowned down at her Venus flytrap familiar then nudged a toad out of his large pot. "Yes, he's back to his old self again after everything that happened." Her voice held a wistful tone, and Issy's heart ached a bit for her cousin who'd been through so much over these past couple of months. "In fact, he's grown so much in the past couple weeks I had to repot him yesterday."

Brimstone hissed then batted a toad away from his tail. "I hope you find Adele's killer soon. All these toads are becoming a nuisance."

Gray shook his head, and his white cockatoo familiar Cosmo flapped his wings to gain better purchase on Gray's muscular shoulder. "Tell me again how Adele's death is related to this amphibian invasion?"

Issy sighed and tucked a strawberry-blond curl behind her ear. "The last thing Adele uttered before she passed over was a curse on Silver Hollow. A plague of toads, to be precise. It won't expire until her killer is found."

"Marvelous." Gray wrinkled his nose and pushed a large toad aside with the toe of his boot. "Any ideas on who her murderer might be?"

"Jerry Blaisdale seems like a viable suspect," Raine said. "We were talking earlier today about how erratic he's been acting lately, casting unintentional spells and having inappropriate emotional outbursts."

"That doesn't necessarily make him a killer," Issy said. "He wasn't the only person visiting Adele for readings. A lot of people in town had regular appointments with her."

"Would she start readings again so soon after Scott's funeral?" Ember asked.

"Maybe she wanted to get back into her routine." Gray shrugged, frowning into the fire. "Lots of people use their jobs to help them forget about their troubles."

"True." Issy narrowed her gaze on the dancing flames. "Motive-wise, Owen thinks Adele must've seen something in one of her scrying balls and a client didn't want her to tell anyone."

"I'm not sure about that." Raine frowned. "If she did see something, why wouldn't that person just kill her right away? Why wait?"

"Good question." Ember stroked Endora's fur. "DeeDee came into Divine Cravings this afternoon and told me Ursula thinks Adele was attacked early this morning, not during her normal business hours."

"Since when do witches have normal business hours?" Brimstone asked, with his usual snarky tone.

"Maybe her killer took time to think about what Adele saw. Maybe the more they thought about it, the more they realized they didn't want it getting around town. Then they came back later to do the deed," Gray offered.

"Well, if Ursula said she was attacked earlier this morning, then for Owen's theory to be right, it would've been a client she saw yesterday. Which leads us right back to Jerry Blaisdale, since he's the one person Mr. Crandall said he saw drive up to Adele's yesterday."

"I'm surprised Adele didn't keep some kind of appointment book for her clients. I use one at Sheer

Magic, and most days it's the only way I keep my sanity," Gray said.

"Better get a new one, then, because I don't think the old one's working anymore," Brimstone said, his hellfire-orange eyes holding a definite twinkle of amusement.

"Funny." Gray gave the cat a flat look then fed Cosmo a Brazil nut. "Not."

The sound of a car engine, followed by the crunch of footsteps on Issy's gravel driveway, made the cousins tense.

"Expecting more company?" Raine asked Issy.

"No." She scowled at the corner of her house. "I can't imagine who that would be."

"Howdy, Quinns." DeeDee rounded the end of the house and walked up to their fire pit. "Having a good evening, I hope."

"Fine." Ember scooted over to make room for their unexpected new arrival. "What brings you here tonight, Deputy?"

"I heard you talking about the case when I drove by and figured I'd pull in," she said, ignoring the question. The Quinns exchanged a look, and DeeDee chuckled. "Don't worry. I wasn't eavesdropping, and I've got extra-good hearing too. Wolf shifter, remember?"

Issy exhaled, forcing her tense shoulders to relax slightly. One could never be too careful these days, but DeeDee was a friend.

"Anyway, I thought maybe we could save each other some trouble," DeeDee said.

"Yeah?" Raine passed her a paper plate and bowl of fresh popcorn. "How?"

"We can make a trade." DeeDee piled her plate high with snacks from the table, threw on a pile of popcorn, and then handed the bowl to Gray. "I saw you talking to Mr. Crandall after you left Adele's. We tried to question him too, but he wouldn't tell us anything. Owen wants to know what he said. So, you tell me your information, I'll tell you mine."

Bella yipped, and Issy smiled. "Mr. Crandall didn't tell us much either, unfortunately. Only that he saw Jerry Blaisdale at Adele's place yesterday afternoon for a reading appointment. Mr. Crandall said he didn't see anyone else come or go."

"No one else, huh?"

"Nope," Issy said.

"Darn," DeeDee said around a mouthful of buttery popcorn. "Well, that won't help us much. Unless Jerry doubled back later to kill Adele, there's no way he could've done it. Ursula put the time of Adele's attack time around three a.m. And with that bright-red car of his, I'd think Mr. Crandall would notice Jerry pulling up in the middle of the night."

"I hate to bring this up," Issy said. "But do you think it might've been one of the homeless people Scott associated with?"

"Owen already thought of that too. Sent officers out to question them about an hour ago." DeeDee finished the last of her popcorn then set her empty plate aside. "We looked for an appointment book but didn't find one at her place."

"It was stolen?" Gray asked.

"Most likely," DeeDee said. "We figure that's why the bookcase was ransacked. They were looking for it."

"Interesting," Issy said as DeeDee stood to leave. "Guess we'll have to find it, then."

DeeDee stopped and turned back to Issy. "Oh, one other thing. Dex Nolan is now officially working with us on the case."

Chapter Six

The next morning, Dex stood in Owen's office at the Silver Hollow Sheriff's Department. Not nearly as impressive as it sounded, the offices were basically one-quarter of one floor of the Silver Hollow municipal building downtown. Owen had another one of his garish Hawaiian shirts on, and Dex had to wonder where exactly the guy managed to find the things in the northern woods of New Hampshire. Hard to believe someone would special-order a blue-and-orange shirt festooned with palm trees and surfboards, but then again, to each his own, he supposed.

"What evidence have you collected so far from the murder scene?" Dex asked as Owen plunked down in his chair and kicked his boat-shoe-covered feet up on his desk. Honestly, the guy looked way more like a surfer than any law enforcement officer Dex had ever seen. "Any suspects in custody?"

"Nope." Owen shook his head, sending his shaggy blond hair dancing around his head. "Not likely to bring any in soon either."

"Why not?" Dex frowned. "I thought you found the murder weapon."

"I did. No fingerprints on the log, though. Appears it came from Adele's own house."

"Which supports my theory the killer didn't go there to murder her." Dex leaned against the edge of Owen's cluttered desk. "If it was premeditated, they would've brought a weapon."

"Not necessarily." Owen narrowed his gaze. "Perhaps the killer did bring a weapon, but then they got into a fight with Adele. In the heat of the moment they picked up whatever was handy—a heavy log—and hit her. Or maybe they were planning on murder and knew they could use the log as a weapon. It works better for the killer if we can't tie the log to them, right?"

Dex sighed. "I guess it's possible. Either way, though, I'd say we're dealing with a person who's not an experienced killer, since they left the job unfinished. Poor Adele lingered for hours before she finally died. Just when help had finally arrived too."

DeeDee walked in, waving to both men. "Hey, guys. Just grabbing some paperwork, don't let me disturb you."

"No problem, Deputy." Dex continued to ponder the case. "What about your whole 'killer being a client' theory? I'm not sure that's valid. What could Adele possibly have told her client that would be bad enough to kill for? She was basically running a fortune-telling scam out of her home. Everybody knows that stuff isn't real."

Owen shrugged. "Some people around here take that stuff really seriously, though. Right, DeeDee?"

"Right, boss." DeeDee glanced from Owen to Dex then back again.

Now that he thought about it, Dex couldn't exactly write Adele off as a fraud altogether. Given the weird stuff he'd encountered in Silver Hollow thus far, maybe Adele Brundage really could see into the future with all her crystal balls. An unexpected pang of sadness filled him. "Too bad Adele couldn't have foreseen her own demise."

Dex looked up to see both Owen and DeeDee watching him.

Oops. He hadn't meant to say that last part out loud.

DeeDee gave him a kind smile. "Unfortunately, it doesn't work like that, at least from what Adele told me. She said she never could see anything about herself or her family. She tried, during Scott's trial. Hoped to get some information to clear him, but it never happened."

"What about her son's homeless friends?" Dex asked.

"I don't think it was one of them. I had my officers go down there last night, and they came up empty." Owen tucked his hands behind his head. "Given Scott's history, he would've been my first suspect. But with him dead, that marks the guy off the list."

"He was accused of murder, right?" Dex asked.

"Yeah. Happened ten years ago in Florida. You know how rowdy those spring break parties get." From the grin on Owen's face, Dex suspected Owen had firsthand experience with just how rowdy things got at those parties. Owen's grin dimmed. "Anyway, things turned bad in this case. A girl was strangled and left naked on the beach. Scott and his friends were seen with the girl earlier that night, and the police pegged him as their number one person of interest. Still, they never presented enough evidence to convict him, and he was acquitted. Poor guy always maintained his innocence, but his public image was forever tarnished." Owen shook his head. "Things only went downhill from there for Scott. He got involved in drugs and lived on the streets for years until his overdose last week. Sad story."

Dex straightened. "Would you mind if I tried talking to some of Scott's friends myself?"

"Not at all." Owen dropped his feet from the desk and stood. "He was living with the homeless group just north of town on the riverbank under the old bridge. You can talk to Jerry Blaisdale too, if you want. His name keeps coming up in relation to Adele."

Chapter Seven

That same morning, Issy unlocked the door to her shop, Enchanted Pets, and stepped inside, only to find three toads following her through the open doorway. Gently, she shooed them back outside, where they squatted on the curb and glared at her angrily as she shut the door in their faces.

Sighing, she tossed her keys on the counter before switching on the lights. She'd noticed several more toads hopping around in her yard this morning and again in the town green across from her shop. Not enough to cause widespread alarm amongst the good citizens of Silver Hollow yet, but enough to be worrisome. They needed to find Adele's killer, and fast.

She and Gray had planned to go talk to Jerry Blaisdale around eleven, which would hopefully give them time to catch the guy before he went to lunch. Jerry was the local mechanic and tended to spend far more time with his cars and engines than he did with people, so they hoped by going directly to his garage, they might catch him off guard and get him to open up about what happened during his last meeting with Adele.

Take Dex, a sweet, singsong voice said inside Issy's head. *Cutie Dex. Cute and courageous, Mommy! We like Dex, Mommy!*

Shaking her head, Issy bent and picked up Bella—who was dancing around her feet and yipping. The little Pom's messages were still hit or miss, and these in particular didn't really help Issy's mission to keep her mind off the sexy FBPI detective.

Much as she hated to admit it, Brimstone was right. Bella's training still had a way to go.

Not that she'd tell him that.

As if on cue, the large charcoal-colored cat strutted by Issy and took his usual perch on the top shelf across the room. Issy would bet money he sat up so high because it gave him the advantage of looking down on everyone else in the room. She loved Brimstone, but man, that feline had an ego that wouldn't quit.

Bella yipped in Issy's arms again and licked her chin, and she kissed the cuddly dog on her furry little head. "You're mommy's good little girl, aren't you, Bella? Yes you are. Yes, you're so good. Such a good girl."

Brimstone rolled his hellfire-orange eyes and commenced his usual busy schedule of grooming and napping while Issy got ready to open her store for the day. Thankfully, the morning ended up being fairly busy, between the new shipment of salamanders and several local paranormal customers coming in to buy a new familiar or two. Even a few tourists stopped in to look around, though the out-of-town crowds were dying down a bit now that summer was over.

Eleven a.m. arrived before Issy knew it, and Gray texted her he'd meet her at Jerry's Auto Body. Apparently he'd gotten stuck finishing up a perm for Mrs. Wiggins, and she was, in his words, "super picky." Raine and Ember had bowed out the night before, saying they'd been away from their shops too much lately, so Issy was on her own to head to the garage.

She waited until her assistant, Hannah, arrived for her afternoon shift, then left Enchanted Pets in her capable hands. Heading back out into the crisp autumn day, Issy double-checked her outfit of jeans, brown sweater, and brown boots, then glanced over at Bella trotting along beside her on her leash. She could've driven but figured why not take advantage of the lovely day. Besides, Jerry's business was just a few short blocks away. The exercise would do her and Bella good.

She passed by Brown Betty parked near the curb and stopped to check her reflection in the side mirror, fussing with her hair and applying a quick coat of lip balm. While she was at Jerry's, she should schedule an oil change. It had been a while since she'd had her ancient pickup serviced, and with winter coming, she wanted to be ready. Plus, it would give her a good excuse for being there.

They walked slowly around the town green, passing The Main Squeeze, Silver Hollow's popular juice bar. She waved to Karen Dixon, the owner, as she walked past. Karen stood behind the counter with Luigi Romano by her side. He worked officially for The Committee, sent by them to keep an eye on all the paranormals in Silver Hollow. Unofficially, he wasn't very good at his job and preferred chasing his dream of opening the best pizza joint in the state of New Hampshire. Based on the line of patrons waiting for one of his slices, he was on his way toward making that dream a reality.

Too bad Issy didn't have time to stop for a juice or a slice of Luigi's delicious pizza today. She checked her watch again then picked up her pace.

Jerry's Auto Body sat on a large corner lot off one of the side streets. The front of the place had two bays for vehicles and a small office to the side. Stacks of new tires and various hoses and pumps littered the small parking lot wrapped around the whitewashed building. Typical garage, the air smelled of oil and gasoline and motor grease. She went to the office first but found no one inside, so she headed through a doorway into the first auto bay.

Issy picked up Bella and covered her delicate ears as a loud, high-pitched whine whistled through the air from some kind of hydraulic, pneumatic tool. Then she spotted a pair of black work boots sticking out from beneath a car hoisted up on a set of jacks.

She waited for the noise to stop then cleared her throat. "Jerry, is that you?"

He wheeled his dolly out from beneath the vehicle and squinted up at her, his blue mechanic's overalls smudged with dirt and grime. Jerry wiped his hands on a rag then struggled to his feet. In his midfifties, Jerry stood several inches shorter than Issy's five feet seven. She had to wonder exactly how he fit under that car, given his large beer belly.

Jerry flashed a small, nervous smile, his teeth white against his reddened skin. "Hello, Miss Quinn. What can I do for you today?"

"Well, I stopped by to schedule an oil change," she said, snuggling a trembling Bella closer.

"Sure thing." Jerry led her back into the office and pulled out his scheduling book. "What day and time would you like?"

"Oh, whatever you have, I can make just about anything work, with enough notice." She stroked

Bella's soft fur and did her best to ignore the little dog's ramblings inside her head. *Where's Dex? Cutie Dex. We should go see Dex. It smells funny in here, Mommy. What's that noise, Mommy? Can we stop at the park on the way home, Mommy? I want a treat, Mommy!*

Yeah, more training was definitely in order.

"How about next week? I've got Wednesday at two o'clock open."

"That should be fine, Jerry. Thank you." Issy watched while he scribbled her information down into his book. "Terrible thing about what happened to Adele Brundage, wasn't it?"

Jerry's hands visibly shook as he wrote. In fact, he pressed the pencil so hard against the paper, the lead snapped. He mumbled something under his breath and grabbed a different pencil. "Yes, yes. Awful."

"You were a customer of hers, weren't you?"

Color drained from his pudgy face. Jerry looked up at her, his dark eyes guarded. "I went over there a few times, yeah. Only to help her with her car, though. She never did none of those readings on me. Those things scare me."

"Huh." Issy shifted Bella to her other arm and frowned. "I spoke to Adele's neighbor, Mr. Crandall. He said he saw you at Adele's house the day before her murder. That you fought with her and left in a hurry, flying down their dirt road like a bat out of hell."

Expression darkening to a scowl, Jerry stepped back from his small, cluttered counter. "What? No. I never fought with Adele. I liked her. We got along just fine. We were friends. Why are you here asking all sorts of questions anyway, Miss Quinn? You working for the cops now or something?"

"No, Jerry. I'm not with the police. I'm just trying to find out what happened to her."

"Well, I don't have to answer your questions, then." Jerry kept backing away, his arms flailing now as his gestures became more animated. Every so often tiny sparks would fly from his fingertips as errant spells were cast. One wave caused the coffeepot in the corner to explode. Another sent a set of wrenches in the auto bay clattering to the ground.

The loud noises caused Bella to jump and twitch in Issy's arms, their mental bond going haywire the more nervous the little Pom became. *What's happening, Mommy? I'm scared, Mommy. This man is angry, Mommy! Cutie Dex. I want to see Cutie Dex! Dex isn't scary, Mommy! We like Dex, Mommy!*

"I think you better go, Miss Quinn." Jerry advanced toward her now, his dark eyes wild. He waved his right arm, and the large potted ficus by the door disappeared in a poof. "I need to get back to work now."

Jerry had her cornered, his arms flailing. She squeezed out from the corner and turned abruptly, running into a wall. No, not a wall. A man. She looked up into the handsome face of Dex Nolan just as he put himself between Issy and Jerry, defusing the tense situation.

"Agent Dexter Nolan. FBI." Dex's calm tone was at odds with Jerry's dark frown. "Is there a problem here?"

Jerry's expression shifted quickly to nervousness. "Uh, no, sir. No problem at all. I was getting Miss Quinn here scheduled for an oil change next week."

"Good." Dex gave the smaller man a cool smile. "Wait here for a moment, Mr. Blaisdale. I have some questions for you. But first I need to speak with Miss Quinn a moment."

"Uh, sure." Dots of crimson returned to Jerry's pale cheeks, and he looked around, anywhere but at Issy.

Still too stunned by the abrupt change in Jerry's demeanor when she'd brought up Adele, Issy remained rooted to the spot.

Dex took her arm and gently guided her outside the office. "Are you all right?"

"Yes, I'm fine." She smoothed a hand down the front of her sweater, doing her best to keep a hold of Bella, who was attempting to leap into Dex's arms. "Thank you for asking."

He crossed his arms, watching her. The movement only served to highlight his beefy arms and broad chest. Issy was grateful he'd stepped in when he did with Jerry, but seeing him again gave her mixed emotions. Part of her wanted to grab him and kiss him silly. The other part of her remembered a relationship between a witch and a mortal would never, ever work.

Torn, she stroked Bella and did her best to tune out her familiar's besotted ramblings. *Cutie Dex! We want to cuddle Dex and snuggle him and stay with him. Can we, Mommy?*

"So," Dex said, breaking the awkward silence. "Involved in another murder, huh?"

He raised a dark brow, his expression curious. His voice was soft and smooth and as inviting as black velvet. Her resolve to steer clear of him softened. Maybe he could eventually accept her as a witch after all. The kisses they'd shared *had* been beyond magical...

This was not helping her situation. Not at all.

She took a step back and squared her shoulders.

Issy couldn't let Dex Nolan distract her. Not now. Not when her friend had been murdered and they had a potential toad apocalypse on the way. "I'm here as a concerned citizen, that's all. I have every right to ask questions."

"Is that so?" Dex's voice grew edgier, and he closed the distance between them once more. "It's not safe, Issy. You need to stay away from potential killers."

Issy inched backward again, only to smack up against the cinder-block wall of the building. "You don't know that Jerry killed Adele."

Dex continued to move closer, until mere inches separated them. "And you don't know that he didn't."

Once more, she was struck by the heat of him, the power of his muscles beneath his dark-blue shirt, the scent of his cedar-and-sandalwood cologne. They were so close now, if she raised up on tiptoe, she could kiss him again. Her lips tingled. As if drawn by an invisible cord, Issy leaned nearer, nearer…

"Sorry I'm late." Gray's deep baritone had her jumping away from Dex.

Heat prickled up from beneath the neckline of her sweater, and Issy kept her gaze steadfastly on the toes of her brown boots.

"No problem," she managed to squeak past her constricted vocal cords.

Dex remained silent.

Gray stepped closer, his tone laced with interest now. "Am I interrupting something?"

"No!" both she and Dex said in unison, each taking another step away for good measure.

She forced herself to meet her cousin's gaze. "I was making an appointment with Jerry, and Dex happened to show up at the same time, that's all."

"Right." Gray looked between the two of them, his expression quizzical. "Sorry again about being late, Issy. Mrs. Wiggins changed her mind about her hair color, and I—"

"It's fine." Issy grabbed Gray's arm and tugged him toward the parking lot. "I was just leaving."

"Issy?" Dex called from behind her. She turned back to face him again then regretted it almost instantly. The concern on his face almost melted her heart. "Be careful around those potential killers, okay? I don't want the next body I see zipped into a bag to be yours."

Chapter Eight

After Issy left, Dex went back inside the office and found Jerry waiting exactly where he'd left him. Dex put on his best official-cop expression and held out his badge. "Agent Dexter Nolan, Federal Bureau of Investigation. I've been assigned to the Adele Brundage murder case, and I need to ask you a few questions, Mr. Blaisdale."

"Oh, um. Sure, okay." Jerry visibly trembled but seemed a heck of a lot meeker than he had when Dex had stumbled upon him with Issy. The thought of this guy hurting her made Dex want to punch a hole through the office wall, but he refrained, keeping his clenched fists by his sides instead.

"Can you tell me where you were in the early morning hours of September twenty-second?" Dex asked.

"At home, in bed." Jerry stepped behind his counter once more, as if using it as a barrier. Body-language-wise, this guy seemed like he had something to hide.

"Any witnesses?" Dex kept his tone flat as he jotted notes in a small notebook.

"No. I was alone." Jerry ran a shaking hand through his salt-and-pepper hair. "I didn't kill Adele, if that's why you're here."

"You were seen at her place the day before the murder. Why were you there?"

"I went to visit her, that's all. We've both lived in Silver Hollow our whole lives, and she was my friend. Her son died last week, and I wanted to make sure she was okay." He gave Dex a suspicious stare. "That's what friends do. They look out for each other. What's wrong with that?"

Dex ignored Jerry's question. "A witness said you left her home rather abruptly, Mr. Blaisdale. Why was that?"

Jerry frowned. "I was late for an appointment. Who told you that anyway? Crandall? He's crazy, you know. Can't trust a word out of that old guy's mouth."

While scribbling his notes, Dex observed Jerry from beneath his lashes. The guy kept twitching nervously like he was a live wire or something. A ceramic cup exploded on the counter, and Dex jumped. Then a loud bang sounded, and both men ducked for cover. Instead of a gunshot, however, the noise was followed by the slow hiss of air. A tire had exploded in the auto bay next door.

Something weird was going on. Dex could feel it. But what exactly it was, Dex had no idea.

"Look, I got work to do, cars to fix. Are we about done here?" Jerry asked.

Considering he was getting nowhere fast with Mr. Blaisdale, Dex nodded. If he needed anything more, he could come back later. "Yes, we're done for now."

"Good." Jerry headed back into his garage without another word.

Dex walked back out to his Buick and climbed behind the wheel, only to get back out quickly. He'd sat on something bumpy, and it was moving. A toad. After removing his unwanted passenger from the vehicle, he got back in, only to find another toad staring at him from the dashboard. What was it with these things? He got rid of that toad too then pulled out of the lot before any more of the creatures found their way inside. He stopped at a red light and glanced in the rearview mirror. Maybe he'd come back to the garage after it closed and poke around some more. Jerry Blaisdale was definitely hiding something.

The light turned green, and Dex accelerated, only to slow down and swerve over to the curb on a side street when his phone rang. He didn't have Bluetooth in his ancient Buick. He pulled out his phone. Stan again.

"What can I do for you, boss?"

"Calling to see if you need me to come down. Did you check out that incident? Any paranormal happenings?"

Dex could honestly say at this point there weren't. Unless, of course, you counted those scrying balls. Which he didn't. "Nope. No evidence of anything paranormal involved at this point."

Stan sounded genuinely disappointed. "Darn. What about the murder? Any suspects?"

After relaying what he'd found out in Owen's office earlier, Dex couldn't help thinking about Jerry Blaisdale again. Weird how that guy kept twitching just before stuff would bust or explode. Oh well. He should be used to that sort of thing by now. Seeing Issy today had been a bonus. Images of them together flooded his mind—at dinner in the next town over, strolling on the boardwalk, kissing beneath the moonlight...

If there was anything magical happening in this town, it was her.

Issy Quinn was magic indeed.

He'd not missed the sparkle of interest in her eyes today or the way she responded to him even as she seemed to deny her attraction. He rubbed a hand over his face and reminded himself of his failure at Enid Pettywood's.

He was a fool. Issy wouldn't want him.

No woman wanted a man who couldn't protect her.

He wrapped up his phone call with Stan then tossed his phone on the passenger seat and glanced in the mirror before pulling out into traffic again. Out of the corner of his eye, he spotted Jerry walking out of the body shop and getting into his red Honda Civic.

Hunching down as Jerry sped past him, Dex straightened and followed his suspect. Several blocks away, Jerry got out and walked over to another car, a white sedan with a rental company sticker on the back.

Dex's outlook brightened.

Apparently Jerry Blaisdale wasn't as innocent as he pretended.

Chapter Nine

"So you went to see Jerry earlier today?" Ember asked as the Quinn cousins climbed out of Raine's Jeep and stood on the berm of the highway, waiting for Raine to lock up the vehicle.

"Yes," she said as she hugged her gray hooded sweatshirt tighter around herself in the chilly autumn evening. Bella was tucked cozily inside to keep her tiny body warm. "Gray got stuck working on Mrs. Wiggins, so I ended up going by myself."

After what Troy and Len had said the other day at Adele's house, they'd all decided speaking directly to some of Scott's homeless friends would be a good idea. Too bad they'd all had to work late at their shops, so they hadn't made it down to the bridge until after sunset. Issy bounced on her heels, trying to generate some extra body heat. The temperatures seemed to have taken a more abrupt dip than usual tonight. Either that or she was just nervous about talking to a bunch of strangers who may or may not have murdered a friend of hers.

Dex's parting words came rushing back to her mind.

Be careful around those potential killers, okay? I don't want the next body I see zipped into a bag to be yours…

Maybe someday she'd heed his advice. Now, however, she had people to question.

"What did Jerry have to say?" Raine asked when Issy didn't elaborate. She'd wisely left Morty at home, given the below-normal temps. No sense shocking the poor plant's system.

"Not much." Issy shrugged. "He got very defensive when I brought up Adele, though, and the fact Mr. Crandall had seen him leaving in a hurry the day before the murder."

"Don't forget the most important part," Gray said, his breath frosting on the air. Cosmo squawked from his shoulder, doing a little cockatoo dance from leg to leg, as if he were trying to stay warm as well.

"What's that?" Issy asked, frowning.

"Dex Nolan arrived to save the day." Gray grinned. "Funny, but I couldn't seem to find his white horse anywhere."

"Stop it." Issy smacked her cousin playfully on the arm, though inside she was mortified. Was her infatuation with Dex so obvious? "Or I'll start teasing you about a certain South Side witch that you seemed to be overly friendly with over the summer."

Gray's jaw tightened and his eyes turned steely at the mention of Starla Knight. A member of a rival coven, they'd had to cross paths with her when they were trying to vanquish the demon that summer. Issy had thought she'd sensed a spark... or something between Gray and Starla. Judging by the look on Gray's face, that subject was taboo, so she continued on. "Besides, Dex walked in as Jerry's little problem with his spells went crazy and things started exploding all over the shop. I had to do something to distract him."

"Right." Gray looked totally unconvinced. "And here I thought you were just about to kiss him when I walked up."

"What?" Ember's pretty face lit with interest. Her kittens, Endora and Bellatrix, meowed softly from inside the fleece-lined basket over Ember's elbow. "I knew you still liked him."

"Enough, guys, okay?" Issy had no problem keeping her cheeks warm now. They felt like they were practically on fire with embarrassment. She shook her head then started down the steep gravel embankment that led under the bridge. "Let's get this over with so I can get home and snuggle under my blankets. I'm freezing."

"Maybe you can call Dex and have him keep you warm," Gray teased, following close behind her.

Once they made it the riverbank, Issy saw a group of about twenty people—men, women, children—all living in a cardboard shantytown harbored against the cement pylons of the bridge. They had several fires going to heat the area, and the air smelled of burnt leaves and roasting potatoes.

Issy and her cousins approached the group slowly and stopped several feet from the nearest fire, hoping for a friendly invitation to join them. Instead, their presence seemed to meet with wary glances and hushed whispers. At least the kids seemed to enjoy meeting their familiars. They rushed over to pet Bella and the kittens and coo to Cosmo, with their parents eventually joining them.

"What can we do for you folks?" one man asked, taking a little boy by the hand. The guy looked about Issy's age, though it was hard to tell with his thick beard and straggly hair. He tugged the boy closer to his side as if to protect him. "You with the police?"

"No," Issy reassured him. "My name's Isolde Quinn. I live in Silver Hollow and run the pet store in town. But please call me Issy. Everyone does."

The man stared at her extended hand for a moment before shaking it. "Ed."

"Hi, Ed. Great to meet you." Issy glanced at her cousins before introducing them as well. "We're here because of what happened to our friend, Adele Brundage."

"I see." Ed's expression remained stoic, though a shadow of sadness flickered through his dark eyes. "Tragic. The whole thing. First Scott and then his mother." He led them to the nearest fire, and they stood around it, warming their hands. "Hard to believe the whole family's gone."

"Yes." Ember reached into her basket. "Oh, I almost forgot. I brought along some chocolates for all of you to enjoy. I run Divine Cravings." She pulled out several large boxes of candy from her enchanted basket and handed them to Ed. "I hope you like them."

"I'm sure we will." Ed hailed over several more people and passed the food around. Soon, the whole little homeless village was sitting around the fire, laughing and enjoying their rare treat. Issy couldn't help but smile too. For people who had so little, they seemed like quite a happy bunch. Soon the conversation turned back toward Scott's death again, though, and the atmosphere took a decidedly sad tone. "Losing Scott was like losing a brother," Ed said. "Around here, we stay close to our own to survive."

"Were there any signs he was so distraught?" Issy asked gently.

"No, not like that." Ed stared at the orange flames leaping out of the top of the metal trash can. "Except for that one day. He got all upset when that lady in the white car came to talk to him. Later, though, Scott's friend that comes here sometimes calmed him down. I thought he was good after that." Ed sniffed and looked away. "We found Scott dead the next morning."

"That's so sad," Raine said, her shoulders hunched beneath her black hoodie. "I'm so sorry that happened to all of you."

"Us too." Ed stood and gestured for the Quinns to follow him. He walked them over to the far corner of the makeshift village and showed them a memorial the folks had set up to honor Scott. "It's not much," he said, "but we wanted to do something to show how much he meant to us."

"It's beautiful." Issy gazed at all the pretty glass beads and trinkets scattered over a large photo of Scott in the middle. "Where did you find all these things?"

"The Dumpster Network," Ed said.

"The what?" Gray asked, his expression puzzled.

"The Dumpster Network." Ed picked up what looked like a small hand-painted ceramic flower. "The homeless around Silver Hollow and a few other nearby towns trade and sell items they find in dumpsters or discarded on the street."

They walked back over to the fire and took their seats. Issy kept close to her cousins, not because she was afraid, but for the body heat. "This whole Dumpster Network sounds really interesting," Issy said. "I never knew that existed."

"Even homeless people need to get new things. Don't got no money for shopping," a man wearing a green army jacket several sizes too big for him said.

Something Ed had said niggled at Issy. "You said someone came here to talk to Scott?"

"Yeah, lots of people coming here. You people. The cops. It's been like Grand Central Station here with visitors," a woman said from the other side of her. She looked younger, maybe early-twenties, and had a pretty face beneath the smudges of dirt and the ratty old knit cap on her head.

This drew several snickers and nods of agreement from the other homeless.

Issy glanced at her cousins, thinking this might be a good lead into the case. "Really? Who else has been here?"

The young woman shrugged. "Like Ed said, that lady in the white car stopped by, though, before Scott..." Her voice trailed off as tears spilled down her cheeks. She sniffled then swiped the back of her hand under her nose. "Oh, and those two friends of Scott, the uppity ones, they was here too. They'd stop by every so often to buy him a good meal. Given how much they paid for that Caddie of theirs, though, they was probably just trying to make themselves feel better by doing it. At least they came by to pay their respects to Marcy. Too bad the cops came and scared her off."

Issy exchanged a did-you-hear-that look with her cousins.

"Who's Marcy?" she asked as casually as she could.

"Scott's girlfriend," Ed said from his spot on the other side of the fire.

"Is she here now?" Ember asked.

"Um." Ed frowned and glanced around at the gathered faces. "No, I don't think she's around at the moment."

"Wait, here she comes," the younger woman beside Issy said. She pointed to the far side of the shantytown.

A thin woman with long, scraggly hair and a navy-blue hoodie with a thick white stripe down the left sleeve was walking toward them past another trash can fire. She looked up and saw everyone pointing at her and froze in place, eyes wide and posture tense.

Issy stood slowly, hoping to speak with her, but before she could take a step, the woman panicked and ran off into the night.

Gray took off down the riverbank after her, but returned moments later empty-handed. He hunkered down beside the fire again and held his hands out to warm them. "She took off into the woods."

"Marcy's been acting kind of spooked since Scott died," Ed said.

"I'm sorry." Gray frowned. "I didn't mean to scare her. We only wanted to talk to her."

"What do you think spooked her?" Issy asked.

"Not sure." Ed shrugged.

"Do you think she might've seen something she shouldn't have where Scott was concerned?" Issy glanced at her cousins then back at Ed. If so, it was the first good new lead they'd gotten.

"Could be," Ed said. "Hard telling with her sometimes."

"Well." Issy stood and gestured for her cousins to do the same. "Thanks so much for letting us share your fire tonight." She pulled a business card from her pocket and handed it to Ed. Not that she expected him to call her. The people here didn't exactly have phones, but maybe the card would remind him to visit her in town. "If Marcy comes back or if you think of anything else that might help us figure out who might've done this to poor Adele, will you let me know? You're welcome at my pet store anytime."

"Sure thing." Ed walked them back to the embankment then turned to Ember. "Thanks again for the chocolate. That was a real treat for the kids."

"My pleasure."

They walked back up the hill to the Jeep, and Raine started the engine and cranked the heat while the others climbed in.

Ed closed the passenger door for Issy and smiled. "You folks come back anytime."

"Thanks." Ember pushed her head through from the backseat to talk to Ed. "I'll be sure to send more chocolates over next week."

"That would be great." Ed thumped the side of the car and looked back at Issy. "I'll be sure to get in touch if we see anything else."

Chapter Ten

The next morning, Dex was at yet another meeting in Owen's office. He pulled up a chair to the sheriff's desk. At least he'd thought to stop and bring doughnuts this time. He sipped his steaming hot black coffee and slumped back in his seat. "So, what's new on the Brundage case?"

DeeDee took a seat at her desk across from Owen's and pulled out her notebook. "I traced the license plate of that white car you saw yesterday, Dex. Seems it was rented to a woman named Linda Brewer. She's a private investigator. I'm running a complete background check now."

"A PI, huh?" Owen said around a huge bite of glazed doughnut. "Why would Jerry be talking to a private investigator?"

"Maybe Adele hired her to look into Scott's death and something came up about Jerry?" Dex offered. He was glad he'd gotten the extra-large coffee today, both for the added caffeine kick and for the steady warmth it provided to his hands. Last night, temperatures had dropped lower than he'd expected this time of year.

Though this far north, nights could be colder than he was used to. He took another gulp of coffee then grabbed a doughnut for himself. "What about Jerry's background check. Anything pop up there?"

"Not really." DeeDee thumbed through the document. "Looks like he was actually a cop himself for a few years back in the day, then he left the force to work as a security guard at Buymart for a year or two. Worked security at the old applesauce plant too, then the paper mill, and the mall over in Franklin, before he opened his body shop about nine years ago."

"Huh." Dex finished his doughnut then wiped his mouth with one of the paper napkins the bakery had provided. "Think maybe he's trying to get back into the security business? That might explain why he met with the PI."

"Not sure." Owen finished the last of his coffee and tossed his empty cup into the trash can beside his desk. "I asked around town yesterday, trying to find out who saw Adele recently for a reading. Three people said they booked appointments, but none of them were suspicious, and their alibis for the night of the murder all checked out. A couple of others said they wanted to make an appointment with her, but Adele had turned them away. Said she wasn't taking on new customers since her son's death. So, it seems like that angle is a dead end."

"Man, this whole thing still doesn't seem right to me." Dex sat forward to throw away his own trash. "My gut tells me this is less about some vision Adele might've seen in her crystal ball, and more about something else. What that something else is, though, I've got no idea."

"Did you go out to question the homeless?" DeeDee asked as she flipped her notebook closed.

"I did. Or at least I tried." Dex frowned. "I was only able to get a few noncommittal comments from some of them. The minute they saw I was a cop, most of them scattered."

"We need to keep on this, but meanwhile we have other crimes to investigate." Owen grabbed a police report out of his inbox. "Someone tried to break in to the funeral parlor last night."

"Seriously?" DeeDee scrunched her nose. "Did they steal anything?"

"Nope. Didn't make it inside." Owen sat back in his chair and propped his feet up on his desk again. "Says here the crooks tripped the alarm and ran away. Who'd want to break in to a funeral parlor?"

"Guess it's better than one of the bodies trying to break out," Dex said, attempting humor.

"Okay." DeeDee stood. "I guess I'll take that one."

Dex pushed to his feet as well. "I'll see if I can track down this Linda Brewer and talk to her. Maybe I'll try to have another chat with Jerry and the homeless folks later too. Too bad we can't round them all up and bring them in for questioning."

"Nah." Owen straightened. "I don't want to do that. Those poor folks have been through enough already in their lives. No need to disrupt what little peace they have any further." Dex shot him an incredulous look, and Owen gave a one-shoulder shrug. "I know, I know. But I've got a soft spot for them. Most of those homeless are nice people, just down on their luck. They never cause any trouble. I don't want to scare them by having them think they're under arrest."

"Fine." Dex headed for the door. "I still think we need to talk to them, though. They might've seen something or heard something from Scott that would help us solve Adele's murder."

DeeDee followed him out. "Don't worry. I have an idea on how we can find out what we need without having to go to extremes."

"Really?" Dex asked as they headed out to the front of the municipal building. "Care to share?"

"Not yet." DeeDee nodded, the gold deputy badge on her chest glinting in the sunlight as she climbed in behind the wheel of her squad car. "But I'll be in touch, Agent Nolan. You have a good day now."

Chapter Eleven

Issy was busy installing a new terrarium for her latest batch of rare purple solstice toads at Enchanted Pets when her phone buzzed in her pocket. Out of habit, more than necessity, she clutched the egg-shaped obsidian talisman she kept tucked away in the same pocket as her cell before pulling out her phone. That talisman had gotten her out of more than one sticky situation recently, and she just felt more secure keeping it close at all times.

"Can you handle this for a minute by yourself?" she asked her assistant. Hannah nodded, and Issy climbed down off her stepladder. Phone in hand, she glanced at the screen and saw a text from DeeDee:

COMPARE NOTES?

KNOW YOU TALKED TO THE HOMELESS.

"Um, Hannah. Would you mind watching the store for a minute?" Issy asked. "I need to run out and see someone for a minute."

"No prob," Hannah said, smiling. She was the best hire Issy had ever made. Faithful and reliable, and she never questioned Issy's odd comings or goings at all hours. In fact, now that she thought about it, Hannah deserved a raise. She'd be sure to add it to her next paycheck as a special bonus for being such a great employee.

"Thank you." Issy grabbed her purse from under the counter and eyed her rainbow-colored hoodie. She'd awakened to find a thin layer of frost on Brown Betty this morning and had grabbed the hoodie for the ride in. But now, the sun had been out in full force, and the day had likely warmed. She probably wouldn't need the extra layer over her long-sleeved T-shirt. She hooked Bella's leash up to her pink harness then took off for the front door. "Be back as soon as I can."

Hannah waved, her head stuck inside the terrarium again.

As Issy hurried across the town green toward The Main Squeeze, she sent out a quick text to her three cousins to meet her at the juice bar as soon as possible. She scurried across the grass, toads hopping out of her way. Bella detoured to chase one.

"Bella, not now."

The dog gave a regretful glance at the toad then trotted back to Issy's side.

The air was crisp but pleasant. One of those perfect fall days that New Englanders loved to take advantage of by sitting outside. Up north, you grabbed any chance you could this late in the season. You never knew when it would be the last time until spring. She ordered a Pineapple Pucker from Karen. It was a new blend of pineapple, celery, kale, and lemon. Supposed to be great for digestion, but Issy just liked the taste.

She took her drink to one of the outside tables positioned in the sun to wait for her cousins. Behind the pizza counter, Luigi cast a suspicious eye her way. Maybe he was just hoping she'd order a slice, but Issy couldn't help but fidget under his constant attention. He probably figured after all the trouble she and her cousins had given him and The Committee—first with Louella Drummond's murder and then with the demon summoning Enid Pettywood had done by accident—his best bet to keep his current position as investigator was to keep a close eye on the Quinn clan.

Luigi leaned on the counter, his long dark hair and scraggly beard looking right at home beside Karen's goth-inspired outfit. She'd begun to wonder if perhaps there'd been something more than a professional relationship brewing between the two. If so, that would be great as it would give Luigi something else to focus on besides scrutinizing Issy and her cousins.

"Hey, cuz," Raine said as she and Ember arrived together, then breezed past to the juice counter with

Gray in close pursuit. The three of them got their juices and then joined Issy at the table.

"What's up? Got new information on Adele's case?" Raine swirled her straw around inside her bluish-green drink.

"Not yet." Issy brushed a meddlesome toad off the tabletop. "DeeDee texted me and said she wants to meet here to swap information."

"That's good." Ember set her basket with her kittens inside on her lap. "Maybe with a little cooperation we can get this thing solved. These toads are getting out of control. I'm having a heck of a time keeping them out of my kitchen at Divine Cravings."

"Tell me about it." Gray arrived and raked a hand through his shoulder-length dark hair. "I went to shampoo a client earlier and one hopped right out of the bowl. Scared her half to death."

"Not to mention they keep damaging all my holiday plants." Raine sat back in her chair and scowled. "If we don't solve Adele's case soon, we're all going to be out of business."

"Howdy, Quinns!" DeeDee said out the open window of her squad car. She parked along the curb then got out and headed for their table. DeeDee took a seat and leaned her elbows on the table. "I know you all went down and talked to those homeless under the bridge."

"How?" Ember asked. "Is Owen spying on us?"

"No." DeeDee smiled. "I happened to drive by and saw Brown Betty parked near the berm. There's no other reason to go down there at that time of night, so I put two and two together. Did you find out anything useful?"

"A bit." Issy nodded. "Scott had a girlfriend."

"Really? Who?" DeeDee asked.

"A homeless girl by the name of Marcy," Gray said. "I tried to catch her to ask her some questions, but she ran away into the woods before I could talk to her."

"You seem to have that effect on women, don't you, buddy?" DeeDee teased, nudging Gray in the arm with her elbow. "Kidding. I wonder why she'd run, though, if she wasn't guilty of something."

"Was she at Scott's funeral?" Raine asked.

"I don't remember seeing her," Issy said. "But there were a lot of people, and I didn't know who they were. She could have been there, and I wouldn't remember. Maybe she was involved in that altercation at the wake, though. Troy mentioned Adele was fighting with one of the homeless."

"Huh." DeeDee frowned and pulled out her small notebook, scribbling Troy's name down in it. "Looks like

I'll be making another trip to Holland Mills to talk to Troy, then. He failed to mention that to me during my initial questioning. Wonder what else he hasn't told me. Did you hear anything else?"

"The homeless guy we spoke with, his name is Ed," Gray said. "He mentioned Troy and Len stopping down to talk to Scott a few times and them buying him a meal every so often."

"No surprise there." DeeDee shook her head. "Those three were always good friends through school."

"True." Gray's dark brows drew together. "But Ed also mentioned a woman in a white car coming to see Scott and Scott being really upset afterward."

"Ah. I know who she is." DeeDee flipped back a few pages in her notebook. "Had a meeting with Owen and Dex this morning, and that white car is apparently being rented by a woman named Linda Brewer. She's a private investigator. I'm getting more background on her now."

"Seriously?" Raine snorted. "Why would a PI be in Silver Hollow talking to homeless people?"

"Don't know yet." DeeDee closed her notebook. "She was also seen meeting with Jerry Blaisdale."

"Jerry? Do you think she's investigating him too?" Gray asked.

DeeDee shrugged and sat back, pushing a toad aside with the toe of her black work boot. "We did a background check on Jerry. Did you guys know he was a cop for a while after high school? Worked in security too for a couple of places in the area. Owen thought maybe he wanted to get back into the security business, seeing as how the auto repair business can't be all that lucrative."

"Huh. Or maybe he's up to something else," Issy said. She glanced inside and spotted Luigi behind the counter again, a long line of customers in front of him waiting to place their orders. Good. That should keep him busy for a while.

"Like what?" Ember asked, cuddling Endora under her chin while Bellatrix hogged the basket. "You said he was acting weird when you talked to him, right, Issy?"

"Weird how?" DeeDee leaned forward again, her gaze narrowed.

Issy took a deep breath. She didn't like to think about that day at the garage because those thoughts led to what had occurred outside afterward. The way Dex had cornered her against the wall and they'd almost shared another kiss, the way he smelled like her favorite woods after a misty rainfall, the way the heat of him surrounded her and warmed her all the way to her bones, the way...

Ember cleared her throat and shot Issy a knowing grin. Everyone else at the table stared at her with expectant expressions. Right. Time to focus on solving Adele's murder and forget about Dex. She gathered her thoughts before answering. "Well, when I asked Jerry about Adele, he got nervous and agitated. Then his magic seemed to go wonky, and he started casting off strange charms and hexes without meaning to. Things around his office were shaking and exploding. Ember told me her customers have been talking for a while about his spells going haywire. Has anyone complained about anything strange when he's around, DeeDee?"

"All the recent complaints we've received have been about the overabundance of toads." As if on cue, several more of the creatures jumped up on their table, croaking loudly. "Unless you count an attempted break-in at the funeral parlor last night."

"Ew." Raine scrunched her nose and shoved the toads off the table. "Why would anyone break in to a funeral parlor?"

"That's exactly what I asked," DeeDee said. "Then I got to thinking on the way over here. That's where Adele's body is being held, isn't it?"

The Quinn cousins all locked gazes.

Issy glanced toward Luigi once more, who was still inside serving up slices of pizza, then lowered her voice.

The man might not be adept at investigating the paranormal around here, but that didn't mean he couldn't cast a simple spell to hear their conversations. "Do you think Jerry's trying to raise the dead with some kind of dark magic? Maybe Adele wanted him to revive Scott or something and now he's in there trying to do the same for her. He told me they used to be friends."

Gray shuddered. "First of all, that's just creepy. Second, we can't go around spouting off wild accusations about dark magic until we're absolutely sure that's what's involved. Remember what happened with Louella's case? It won't do anyone any good if Luigi gets wind of the information then goes sticking his nose into things again. We've already got enough people investigating this case. And besides, *why* would Jerry want to do that?"

"Good point." Issy glanced inside the juice bar and caught Luigi watching them again, his expression suspicious. She waved, hoping to distract him. He returned the gesture but continued to stare at their table anyway. For a man who was supposedly not very good at his job as watcher, he was sure being persistent today.

She shook off her reservations and refocused on their conversation at hand.

"Sorry." Ember put Endora back in the basket and picked up Bellatrix to cuddle instead. "I still don't understand how this PI lady fits into all of this."

"It would help to know why this Linda Brewer is here in Silver Hollow and who she's investigating," Issy said.

"Pretty sure your Dex is working on that now. He planned on going to talk to her later today, I think." DeeDee checked her notebook yet again, grinning at Issy over the top. "If you hurry, you might run into him."

"He's not *my* Dex," Issy said, doing her best to keep the irritation from her tone and failing miserably, if her cousins' smirks were any indication. "Besides, I wouldn't want to bother him while he's working."

"I'm sure it would be no bother at all, cuz." Raine winked.

Heat warmed Issy's cheeks, and her lips tightened. "I told you guys things would never work out between us. Leave it alone already."

"Aw, that's too bad." DeeDee looked up at Issy, her smile widening. "Dex has seemed kind of lonely lately. I always thought there seemed to be a spark between the two of you. If that's the case, Issy, you shouldn't pass that up." DeeDee's amused expression turned serious. "Remember, not everyone is lucky enough to have the choice of who they want to marry."

Issy winced. "How are things going with your father's arrangement?"

"Arranged marriage, you mean." DeeDee shook her head, her perfectly coiffed auburn locks—a la Gray—dancing around her head. "Not good. Dad's on a retreat up north with his new wife, so they're out of communication range, but they've moved up the date for the wolf packs to merge. That's about all I know at this point. Other than my single days are coming to an end in January."

"I'm sorry." Ember reached across and took the deputy's hand. "That stinks. Everyone should be free to choose who they want to love and spend the rest of their life with." Ember leaned to the side and peered past DeeDee, her emerald eyes full of interest. "Speaking of love... who is *that*?"

Issy swiveled in her seat to see an extremely hot, tall, muscled stud with a thick mane of dark-brown hair strutting down the sidewalk on the other side of the town green. She'd never seen him before, which meant he was either new to the area or just passing through on his way elsewhere. Still, he was nice eye candy. Judging from the way DeeDee was currently gaping at the guy, she apparently thought so too, at least until she caught herself and turned back around, scowling.

"Oh, that guy." DeeDee wrinkled her nose, her tone dripping with distaste. "He's some high-maintenance movie producer by the name of Caine"—she gave a dismissive wave—"something or other. We've gotten complaint calls about a few disturbances on his sets. If you want him, Ember, you can have him. He's not my type at all." She crossed her arms and exhaled. "Be careful, though. He's too full of himself, thinks he's a gift to womankind. Plus, he's got a different blonde on his arm every day. He's a real player, from what I can tell."

"Interesting." Ember's gaze remained on DeeDee, not the new stranger in town. "What kind of movie would they film in Silver Hollow?"

"Got me." DeeDee shrugged and stared at the tabletop. "From what I've heard, he's thinking about moving his operations here, so whatever it is, it must be big. I hope it doesn't work out, though. If you ask me, all those flashy sets and cameras bring in a bunch of riffraff."

"Why Silver Hollow though?" Raine frowned. "I mean, it's pretty here, but hardly Hollywood quality."

"Caine specializes in werewolf and vampire movies," DeeDee said, her tone flat.

"Oh," Issy said, her gaze narrowing on DeeDee. The good deputy was a werewolf shifter herself, so perhaps things between her and this new producer wouldn't be so cut and dried after all. "Well, then Silver Hollow would be perfect." Where better to film werewolf and vampire movies than a town that was full of the real thing?

DeeDee made a show of putting away her notebook and pushing to her feet. "I need to get back to the station."

Issy kissed Bella's head then put her down on the ground and stood too. "Anyone else have anything to add?"

"Nope." Ember tucked Bellatrix back into the basket beside Endora then slipped her sunglasses back on. "I need to whip up a new batch of fudge this afternoon, so I best get back to my shop."

"I've got a new shipment of pansy orchids due in today I need to enchant with relaxing magic." Raine followed Ember out onto the sidewalk. "Need to make sure I'm toad-free before they arrive."

Gray stood as well, Cosmo squawking on his shoulder. "We'll wait to hear more from you about this Linda person, eh, DeeDee?"

"Yeah." DeeDee slipped on her aviator shades. "Try not to get more involved in Adele's case than you already are, Quinns. Things could get dangerous."

Chapter Twelve

After DeeDee left, Issy headed back to Enchanted Pets with Bella and Gray by her side. She couldn't help scratching Cosmo on his head as they walked down the sidewalk. "Who's a good birdie, huh? Cosmo is. Yes, sir. Cosmo is such a handsome boy." The bird did a little dance on Gray's shoulder then preened his lovely crown of yellow feathers. Issy laughed. "I figured you had another busy afternoon at Sheer Magic."

"I do." He walked her across the street. "But it won't kill me to take a little break and get out in the fresh air for a minute with my cousin."

"Okay." They walked into the grass on the town green so Bella could chase another toad. "I wonder where that PI DeeDee mentioned is staying."

"Good question." Gray tilted his head and whispered something to Cosmo then released the bird to fly high over their heads. "I told him to keep a lookout for any unfamiliar white cars in the area."

"If we find her, maybe Raine can lend us one of those relaxing orchids." Issy shifted her weight while

Bella started to sniff the ground and twirl in endless circles.

"Dabbling in illegal magic these days?" Gray asked, cocking a dark brow.

"No." Issy gave him an exasperated stare. "I don't mean enough to make the woman do anything against her will or anything. Just enough to relax her and get her to open up about why she's here."

Cosmo returned a few minutes later, swooping back down onto Gray's broad shoulder in an elegant arc. The bird leaned over and nuzzled Gray's ear then began preening again.

Gray nodded then smiled. "He says she's staying over at the Route Nine Motel."

Issy grimaced. The Route Nine was out of the way, built in a swampy area on the outskirts of Silver Hollow. "Not exactly the nicest accommodations around."

"No. But that could work in our favor." Gray cooed to his pet then narrowed his gaze on Issy. "You in a hurry to get back to work?"

She checked her watch. "My assistant Hannah's scheduled until three. Why?"

"Want to go see this Linda Brewer now? If her car is at the motel, then our chances are good she's there too."

"What about Raine's orchid plant?"

"We can swing by her place on the way over."

"Sounds good. Let's take my car." Issy fished her keys out of her pocket and led the way to Brown Betty. Pulling out into traffic with Cosmo sitting on Gray's shoulder right in her line of vision was tricky, but somehow she managed. On the way, they passed Jerry's Auto Body. No cars were in the lot. The windows were dark. "Wonder what that's all about?" Gray asked.

"Maybe he got spooked with all the questions yesterday," Issy said.

Gray twisted in his seat, his eyes fixed on the auto body shop. "Maybe. You did say he was acting nervous. If he is the killer, he might have hightailed it out of town."

"Maybe Linda Brewer will be able to tell us something about him." Issy pulled up in front of Raine's shop, and Gray hopped out to collect the plant.

Twenty minutes later, they were chugging down the highway heading toward the Route Nine Motel. Weak sunshine streamed through the overcast sky, and with each mile they traveled, the air thickened with the smell of stagnant water and decaying plants as they neared the swamp. More toads than ever hopped out onto the roadway in front of Issy's pickup, and she had to swerve several times to avoid squishing them flat.

At last, they pulled into the parking lot and got out, leaving Bella and Cosmo to wait inside the truck. A white rental sedan was parked out front of Room 127. Gray held Raine's enchanted orchid beneath his arm as they walked up to the door and knocked.

A woman in her late twenties answered, her gaze suspicious as she peeked at them from around the security chain. "What do you want?"

Issy forced her brightest smile. "Hello, my name's Isolde Quinn, and this is my cousin, Gray Quinn. We're business owners here in Silver Hollow, and we were hoping we might talk to you for a moment."

The woman squinted at Issy then eyed the plant under Gray's arm. "What's that for?"

"Oh," Gray said then held out the orchid. The purple markings in the center of the five white petals gave the impression of a happy face waving in the slight breeze. "It's a welcome gift for you."

"I don't want any gifts. I didn't move here, just passing through." She tried to close the door, but Issy wedged her toe inside.

"Please, Ms. Brewer," Issy said, crossing her fingers behind her back. "We're friends of Jerry Blaisdale."

The door opened a bit wider again. "How did you know my name?"

Fingers still crossed, Issy glanced at Gray then told another small fib. "Jerry told us."

A few tense moments passed in silence, then a metallic swish sounded as Linda slid the security chain free, allowing them into the motel room.

"Where is Jerry?" Linda asked.

"What do you mean?" Issy exchanged a concerned look with Gray then followed him inside.

Gray set the enchanted orchid on the dresser. "We thought he was still here in town, but his shop was closed when we drove by."

"He told me he was going on vacation." Linda took a seat on the edge of the olive-and-orange floral-covered queen-sized bed near the dresser. The sweet scent of the orchid soon drifted around the small motel room, and Linda's shoulders visibly relaxed. Issy and Gray exchanged a relieved look. "It was all rather sudden. He didn't tell me where he was going, and I really need to talk to him. Are you with the police?"

"No." Issy took a seat in one of two chairs in the room. "We aren't with the police."

"Why should I talk to you then?" Linda asked, her tone less edgy than before. "I already talked to one cop earlier. Nice-looking guy too. His name was Dex."

Gray winked at Issy, and she bit the inside of her cheek to keep from smacking him.

"We know things the police don't," Issy said. "We might be able to help you find Jerry."

Linda seemed to mull this over for a moment then stood and walked over to the dresser. She opened the top drawer and pulled out a folder before bending and sniffing the orchid deeply. "This plant smells wonderful. What kind of orchid did you say it was?"

"Pansy," Gray said, meeting Issy's gaze again. "We're glad you like it, Ms. Brewer."

"Oh, it's lovely. Thanks again for bringing it over. Such a nice gift. And please, call me Linda."

She took a seat on the bed again, and Issy moved her chair closer while Gray grabbed the other chair and placed it beside Issy's.

"So," Issy said. "What's in the folder?"

"Ah." Linda flipped open the file and pulled out several documents, which she handed to Issy. "These are the court transcripts from the trial where Scott Brundage was accused of murdering Sarah Landers. I never believed Scott was guilty, and now I'm here to prove it."

Issy frowned. "This happened a decade ago. Why are you so interested now?"

Linda flinched and looked away. "I just like to see justice done."

Issy glanced at Gray. The woman was hiding something, but she didn't want to press her. Pressing her might get them kicked out before they got a look at the documents.

"Anyway." Linda shrugged. "You're right. It was a long time ago, but back when it happened I was fascinated with the case. I lived around here then, and it was big news. I guess maybe I was always meant to be a PI because something about the whole business seemed off. Then some things they brought up at the trial didn't make sense, and I started to suspect some of the evidence was suppressed or people had been paid off to lie about Scott. His acquittal only helped to prove my point. All of the evidence was too contradictory, too circumstantial. And once I got my PI license I could see there was nothing that conclusively proved Scott Brundage was the real killer."

"Why come to Silver Hollow now, though, after all this time?" Issy asked. "And what does all of this have to do with Jerry?"

Issy got the whole wanting to see justice thing, but why would Linda investigate this on her own dime? Surely she had paid cases to work on. Unless someone was paying her to investigate. Maybe Adele had hired her, and that was why she avoided the earlier question. She might not want to reveal who her client was.

"Over the years I've made some contacts with the police departments involved in the original case," Linda said. "One of the departments recently gave me access to some of the evidence in the case I wasn't allowed to see earlier. In one of the bags were old photos from the last day Sarah spent at the beach. One of the people in the photos was holding a vintage Polaroid instant camera, you know the ones where the picture comes out the front and develops while you wait?"

Issy and Gray both nodded.

"Well, I know it sounds crazy, but I couldn't help thinking maybe whoever had that camera might've captured something the rest of the pictures taken that day missed. All the photos at the trial were digital, and there weren't many of those to boot, since someone threw all the cameras from that day into the pool during a wild party." Linda frowned. "Anyway, when I showed the picture with the Polaroid camera to Jerry, he recognized the model. Said he was some kind of vintage-camera buff."

Issy glanced at Gray then back to Linda. "Did you show that photo to Scott Brundage as well?"

"I did." Linda hugged her arms around her middle. "I went down to that homeless settlement under the bridge and went over the events of Sarah's death with him again. Problem was he couldn't remember what happened. He claimed he'd blacked out most of the trip. Given the drugs Scott was on that last day, he was even confused about who was there on that trip with him ten years ago. I feel bad about that now. Turns out he killed himself that night. Maybe if I didn't dredge all this up, he wouldn't have done that." Linda shook her head. "Made me more determined than ever to find the real killer, and that's why I went to see Jerry Blaisdale. I knew from the original trial that he'd known Adele for years and had spent time around Scott back then. I thought perhaps he could give me more insight into Scott's frame of mind back then, his habits, how much and what kinds of drugs he was taking."

"Did you find anything else interesting in those evidence bags?" Gray asked.

The smell of the orchid was thick in the air now, and Issy rubbed her nose to keep from sneezing. The relaxation spell wouldn't affect her and Gray—Raine had taken special precautions—but the cloying, sweet odor was starting to give Issy a headache just the same. Linda, however, seemed nearly catatonic, sprawling out on her bed and smiling at them serenely. At this point, Issy left all pretense behind, knowing chances were good Linda wouldn't remember this conversation in the morning. "Linda, did you find anything that could give us a clue to who killed Adele Brundage?"

Linda stretched then yawned before pulling out another photo and handing it to Issy. "This was the only other new picture I found in the evidence."

Frowning, Issy stared down at the image of a visitor's badge from Holland Mills. She passed it to Gray. Finally, something new they could go on.

"When I showed that to Jerry," Linda continued, "he said he'd signed Scott into the mill the day before he left to go on the trip. Jerry was working security for the Hollands back then. He said Scott went to the mill to see Troy and Len, who were interning there that spring. I asked him if he'd thought Scott was under the influence of any illegal substances at the time, but Jerry couldn't remember. It was a long time ago."

Gray laid the photo back on Linda's bed then pushed to his feet and moved his chair back to the corner of the room where he'd gotten it. "We need to be going."

"Yes." Linda rubbed her eyes. "I'm so tired all of the sudden."

"Right." Issy grabbed Raine's orchid plant from the dresser before joining Gray near the door. Best to cover their tracks by not leaving enchanted plants around for Luigi to find, in case he was looking. He wasn't known for being particularly adept at his snooping, but they couldn't be too careful these days. She and her cousins were already on The Committee's radar. "Thanks for speaking with us. We'll see what we can find out about Jerry."

Linda rolled off the bed and shuffled over to let them out, frowning at the orchid. "I thought that was a gift?"

"It is, but, umm... I remembered it needs a special plant treatment at my cousin's shop. See how it's all droopy? She'll fix it right up, and I'll bring it back after," Issy said. Maybe she could use that as an excuse to make a return trip should she have more questions for Linda.

"Oh, okay. If you find Jerry, will you let me know? He's been helping me a lot with the case." She chuckled. "Turns out he's studying to be a PI. Did you guys know that? I didn't know until I came here to question him. Small world, eh?"

Issy and Gray exchanged another look as they stood in the open doorway.

"There is one more thing," Issy said. "After you talked to Scott that last day, did he mention where he was going afterward?"

"Hmm." Linda slumped against the doorframe, her eyes heavy-lidded. "Pretty sure he said he was going back to his mom's place to see if there was anything she'd saved from the time of his trial." She frowned and squinted. "Yeah, I remember now. He said he knew Adele had kept stuff in boxes from when he was a kid all the way through his high school and college days. He said his mom would be surprised to see him, since he didn't go home much anymore. Too ashamed of being a homeless drug addict and all. Then he died." She hugged herself tight again. "So sad how that all turned out."

"Very sad," Issy said, her chest aching for Scott and Adele.

"I stuck around to see if I could speak to Adele after the funeral. I was waiting a respectable period of time. I wanted to see if she'd let me look through those boxes Scott said she kept. Now that she's been murdered, I'm guessing whatever's in them must have been pretty important. Important enough to kill for, it seems."

Chapter Thirteen

"Wait," Raine said. "So, Jerry's studying to be a PI too?"

"Yep." Gray leaned his shoulder against the cinder-block wall of the greenhouse. They'd stopped by to drop off her orchid plant. "That's what Linda Brewer *said*, anyway. She said Adele was holding some information back from the days of Scott's trial. My guess is whoever ransacked Adele's bookcases was looking for whatever was in those boxes."

Issy took a deep breath, glad to smell fresh air and dirt again after the thick floral fragrance in Linda's motel room. "And that means Adele's murder might have had nothing to do with her scrying balls or something she told a client. I can't imagine what kind of evidence she would've had, though. Do you think the killer actually found it, or is it still at the house somewhere?"

"Don't know." Gray frowned. "The fact Jerry suddenly left town doesn't look good. Especially since he'd spoken to Linda and knew that stuff was probably hidden somewhere in Adele's house. Too bad we have no idea where he went."

"Can we even trust what Linda told us?" Issy asked. "She was obviously hiding something, and why would she be interested in this old case now anyway?"

Gray pressed his lips together. "Good question. She looked about the same age as Scott…"

"You don't think she might have been involved back then?" Raine asked.

Gray shrugged. "I don't know. What other reason would she have to be looking into it?"

Issy turned to Raine. "Did you put a truth charm on that orchid or just a relaxation?"

"Just relaxation."

"So she could have been lying. There was no charm to compel her to tell the truth," Issy said. "We know she really is a private investigator, but maybe she's here for more personal reasons, and maybe she didn't come to see Jerry for the *exact* reason she told us."

"Right. She could have known that Jerry had information. For all we know she was lying about him going on vacation to cover up," Gray said.

"Cover up what?" Raine asked.

"The fact that she did something to him. What if Linda knew something about the killer, or what if Linda *is* the killer. And she knew that Jerry knew something.

And that something could incriminate her in some way," Gray said.

"If that's the case, what she said about visiting Scott might not have been the whole truth either." Issy's blood chilled. "She admitted to being there the day he died. But what if he wasn't alive when she left?"

"You mean she killed him and staged a suicide?" Raine asked. "But why?"

"I have no idea. Maybe something new came to light recently and she was afraid the case would be reopened?" Issy said.

"If Jerry really was studying to be a PI, maybe it wasn't Linda that requested a meeting with Jerry. Maybe it was the other way around," Gray said.

"Jerry and Adele were friends. He might have started looking into the case. Adele might have even asked him to look into it, which could explain him speeding away from her house and possibly even the fight at the wake. He might have had information she didn't want to hear, or maybe he was trying to persuade her to show him what was in those boxes and she refused," Raine said.

"Or maybe she did show him, and that's how he got Linda's name," Issy suggested.

"But why would Linda come all the way out here? Wouldn't she just blow him off if he contacted her about the murder?" Raine asked.

"Not if she thought he might have evidence against her," Gray said. "She'd come out here and try to get rid of it. And with her PI skills, it wouldn't be that hard."

"Then again, Linda could be on the up and up, and Jerry could have been involved in that death somehow and has skipped town now that he knows Linda is looking into it," Issy said. "He was acting awfully suspicious when I talked to him."

"Either way, we need to look into Jerry's disappearance," Gray said.

"I'm pretty sure Ember has friends who work at the airport." Raine frowned. "I'll call her, and maybe she can check around and find out where Jerry went and if he's really on vacation."

"Good idea." Issy checked her watch. "I need to get back to my shop. Poor Hannah's working overtime as it is."

"Yeah, me too." Gray scrunched his nose. "Mrs. Wiggins is coming back in this afternoon for a color adjustment."

"Do you guys want to get together later and check out Adele's place for ourselves? See if we can find this supposed evidence?" Raine asked.

For the first time since the whole demon-possession mess, excitement sparkled in her eyes, and Issy's hopes soared. The thought her beloved cousin might finally be emerging from her fog of sorrow and depression made her set her cautious instincts aside. If digging deeper into Adele Brundage's murder case brought Raine back to her old self again, Issy would gladly risk anything. "Sounds good. Say right after closing at six thirty tonight?"

They all went their separate ways.

By the time five fifty rolled around, however, Bella was sending urgent telepathic messages Issy's way, saying they needed to get to Adele Brundage's. Her cousins weren't due to close their shops for another forty minutes, but from the way her little Pom was scampering around Issy's feet, this couldn't wait.

Hurry, Mommy! Adele's now! Hurry, hurry!

With a sigh, Issy picked up Bella then grabbed her bag from beneath the counter. It wouldn't hurt anything to close a little early, and business had been slow this afternoon anyway. Besides, she'd been working with Bella on her communication skills. To ignore her familiar's messages now wouldn't help her training at all.

Brimstone stretched lazily from his usual perch on the top shelf then jumped down to join Issy by the front door. "Leaving early, are we?"

"Bella says we need to go to Adele's house now to investigate." Issy held the door for Brimstone then followed him out of Enchanted Pets, turning to lock the door behind them. "I don't want her to think her messages aren't important."

The cat gave an imperious sniff then slowly walked away, nose high in the air. "Considering it's the first time that little pup has done anything of any value, I must say I agree."

Issy watched Brimstone walk away, shaking her head, before heading to the old pickup and securing Bella inside. "Don't listen to him, sweetie. Mommy's very proud. Yes, she is." She kissed the little Pom's head before closing the passenger side door and jogging around the front of the truck to climb behind the wheel. "Off to Adele's we go."

The drive didn't take long, but the sun set early these days, and the woods looked ominous. She turned down the old dirt road and traveled deeper into the forest, the gathering gloom making the whole area seem more scary and spooky than she remembered.

Bella sat in the passenger seat, looking out the window and panting excitedly. Her running commentary full of eagerness.

Tall. Dark. Good! Tall. Dark. Good! TallDarkGood!

She'd done the same thing a few weeks earlier when Luigi had been around, Issy recalled. At least Issy had thought it had been in conjunction with Luigi, since he was tall and dark. The good part was still up for debate. Still, that didn't make much sense now. Why would Luigi Romano be at Adele's house? The murder case didn't have anything to do with him. Or maybe the little dog was commenting on the looming pine trees surrounding them. It was hard to tell these days, since the only subject her familiar seemed to home in on with any clarity was Dex.

And he was the last thing she needed to focus on right now.

After switching on her headlights, Issy quickly pulled into the long dirt drive leading to Adele's place and parked Brown Betty. There were no other cars around, which was a good sign. Even better, another indication there was no Luigi either. She cut the engine and climbed out then walked around to get Bella, ignoring the Pom's stream of telepathic nonsense words.

The little dog immediately began pulling on her leash, seemingly desperate to get inside Adele's door. After locking the truck, Issy walked up onto the porch and tried the knob. Locked, of course. She sniffed the wood around the lock. No waxy smell, meaning another paranormal had not been there to unlock it.

Bella continued to scratch at the wood as Issy ran her fingers over the knob then sucked in a breath. She focused all her supernatural powers, picturing a key fitting into the lock and turning. Fist clenched, Issy unfurled her fingers at the same time she muttered, "*Infero.*"

Snick.

The old door creaked open, and Issy inched inside. A funny tingle started low in her belly, but she pushed it aside. The air smelled stale and musty, undisturbed, like all the life had been sucked out of the house. She fumbled in the darkness, searching for a light switch.

Crash!

Issy swiveled fast toward the kitchen, her breath caught in her throat and her pulse racing. Bella jumped in her arms then shook all over.

Badbadbadbadbadbadbadbadbad!

Through the dim moonlight filtering through the windows, Issy glimpsed a shadow rushing out the back door. Holding tight to Bella, she crept toward the kitchen, only to find the back door busted in. Near the tree line, the intruder darted through a bright patch of moonlight, and Issy saw a flash of a dark-blue hoodie with a white stripe down the sleeve.

Marcy!

"No!" she yelled from the back stoop of Adele's home before taking off down the steps. "Wait!"

She was so preoccupied with catching the homeless girl that she failed to notice the wall of male muscle stepping into her path and collided smack into the solid chest of Dex Nolan.

Chapter Fourteen

"Do I even want to know what you're doing here?" Dex asked, peering down at the top of Issy's strawberry-blond head. After the shock of the abrupt impact, it had taken him a moment to realize who had run out of Adele Brundage's residence and smack into him. Now that he had Issy's warmth in his arms, though, he could honestly say he didn't mind a bit.

Who had she been chasing? Whoever they were, they were still out there, in the woods behind him, and they could be armed and very, very dangerous.

Issy started to step away from him, but Dex tightened his arms around her, keeping her right where she was. He'd not gotten a good look at whomever it was she was chasing but had seen enough of their shabby, dirty clothes to peg them as a member of the homeless group down by the river. The last thing he needed right now was Issy running off into the woods after some vagrant and getting hurt.

She struggled against his hold a bit at first then went limp, keeping her gaze averted and her head lowered.

"How did you get into Adele's?" he asked, to break her continued silence. "Last time I checked, the front door was locked, and the way you came bursting out the back, I don't think that that's the way you got in."

Maybe she picked the lock, he supposed. Then again, given the magical things he'd seen her do at Enid's place, maybe she'd just cast a spell. He wouldn't have been surprised or dismayed. Heck, the way this case was going currently, a little magic could come in handy.

They stood near the edge of the woods, their breath frosting in the chilly evening air, those darned toads hopping around their feet, and yet Dex couldn't have brought himself to move, even if a thousand wild horses stampeded in his direction.

Issy finally looked up, though not at him. Instead she stared at the thick trees beside them. Her tiny dog was snuggled in Issy's arms between them, sniffing Dex's shirt and looking happy as a clam. "That person I was chasing was Scott Brundage's girlfriend. We need to find her and question her about what she knows."

She tried to free herself again, but Dex held fast. "Leave her. If she's with the homeless group, then we know where to find her. Running into those woods at night is too dangerous."

Exhaling, Issy met his gaze at last, her expression speculative. "What are you doing here?"

"Probably the same as you," he said. The longer he held Issy, the more distracted he became. It was harder to concentrate on what she was saying and ignore the heat of her warming him all the way to his toes. "Why?"

"Aren't you going to tell me to stay out of it?" she asked, arching a brow at him. Was it his imagination, or was her voice a tad huskier than before?

Dex forced words past the growing constriction in his throat. "Yes. But first I want to know why you've been avoiding me."

He'd already run through pretty much every possible scenario in his head and had a good idea of her answer. That didn't mean the rejection wouldn't sting when Issy told him she wasn't interested, when she said he was a failure, a fraud, a man who couldn't protect what was his... He closed his eyes and braced for the worst.

"What?" she asked, her tone incredulous. "I thought *you* were avoiding *me*."

Squinting one eye open, Dex scrunched his nose. "Me? Why would I want to avoid you?" He frowned down at her. "From what I recall, we had a great date and then... well, then that *thing* happened and—"

"Yeah, that *thing*." Issy looked away again, and Dex missed the heat of her gaze immediately. "You saw what I am that night, Dex. A witch, a paranormal. Why haven't you taken me in yet?"

"In?" Stunned, he loosened his hold on her slightly. "You mean to Area 59? I wouldn't do that. That place is nasty."

"Right." Issy stepped back, and this time he let her go. "You know what, Dex? Let's just be honest with each other. Just once. I know you saw weird things at Enid's house. I know you're here as an FBPI agent and your job is to report all things paranormal. We both know you remember what happened, so why haven't you performed your sworn duty and reported what you saw?"

Dex crossed his arms and scowled at Issy in the moonlight, a small muscle ticking near his clenched jaw. "Maybe because I don't want them doing a bunch of crazy testing on you or any of the other paranormals around here. I told you the real reason I joined the division that night at the restaurant. About that child, the kidnapping victim, who died because of me, because of my failure to solve the case in time. I will never fail to protect those in my charge like that again. Ever. And if that means keeping a bunch of innocent paranormals from being dragged into Area 59 simply because of who and what they are, then so be it."

Issy blinked at him, eyes wide. "I thought you didn't believe in paranormals."

"I don't... well, I mean I didn't. But now after seeing what you and your cousins can do, I can hardly deny it, can I?"

They stared at each other across the brief expanse of space separating them.

Finally, Issy exhaled slowly, her beautiful gaze earnest. "So that's why you aren't going to turn us in?"

"That." Dex reached for her and pulled her close once more, his lips mere millimeters from hers as he whispered, "And this."

***

Stunned, Issy just stood there, enjoying the feel of Dex's soft, warm lips. She forgot all about Adele's case. Forgot about all her protests that witch-human relationships never worked. Forgot about everything really, except the feel of Dex's strong arms holding her close and the smell of his sandalwood cologne drifting around her, making her feel safe and secure and wanted…

Time lost all meaning as Issy slowly twined one hand around Dex's neck, sinking her fingers into the soft, dark curls at the nape of his neck. Honestly, she could've stood there all night just kissing him and been perfectly content. Even the constant low croak of the toads didn't bother her. In fact, it all seemed rather comforting…

"There you are," Raine said, walking up to them. "Gray and I've been looking all over for you, cuz."

Issy and Dex flew apart fast, each looking around at anything but each other.

Raine's gaze flickered between them, and her smile deepened. She shifted Morty's pot from under one arm to the other then called toward the back door of Adele's house. "Gray, Em! They're out here, near the tree line."

"Who's they?" Gray said, pounding down the back stoop with a scowl on his handsome face. Ember trailed out after him, Endora and Bellatrix peeking wide-eyed at the scene from over the top of their basket. In Gray's hand was one of Adele's walking sticks, which he brandished like a weapon. "That back door is busted out." He squinted at Issy. "Surely you didn't do that."

"Of course not." She fiddled with the zip on her hoodie, making sure Bella was still warm and secure. "I was inside the house, and I saw someone in the kitchen. Turns out it was Marcy, but she ran into the woods before I could catch up with her."

Gray looked at Dex, Cosmo squawking loudly on his shoulder. "Where were you when all this was going on?"

Dex met Gray's hard stare with one of his own. "In case you've forgotten, I'm the only one of this group who's actually supposed to be here. I could have all of you arrested for trespassing and interfering with a crime scene."

"Please, Dex." Issy placed a hand on his forearm, hoping to defuse the suddenly tense situation. The last thing she needed tonight was to go bail Gray out of jail—or worse, for the FBPI to get their hands on him. Dex might have said he was on their side, but the rest of his department couldn't be trusted. "We're all on the same side here. My cousins and I came to search for evidence from Scott's trial we think she might've kept here in the house. Evidence that could have gotten Adele killed."

"Where'd you get your information?" Dex asked, his hazel gaze concerned. "I told you to be careful. I don't want to see you hurt, Issy."

Raine shivered in the chilly night air. "Maybe we could continue this conversation inside? Morty and I are turning blue over here."

After several awkward moments and more tense stares between Dex and Gray, they all made their way back inside Adele's home. While the guys worked to get the back door secured to keep any more would-be snoopers out, Raine, Ember, and Issy rummaged through the bookcases in the living room.

"Looks like this is where Marcy was searching too," Issy said, taking in all the mess and the clean, finger-sized streaks through the otherwise dusty shelves. "Not sure what we're even looking for."

"I saw a picture of Adele in this very room in the newspaper once," Ember said, removing a stack of papers from the shelf. "These bookcases were packed full. Maybe if we straighten up and put everything back, it will reveal what's missing."

"Couldn't hurt," Raine said, shrugging.

The girls stuffed the shelves once more, using the dust outlines left behind to figure out what objects had been where. By the time they were done, they discovered an empty gap of about fifteen inches where something had been, but they had no clue as to what.

Issy wrinkled her nose. "Well, whatever it was, it was definitely bigger than one appointment book."

"Maybe they took more than just an appointment book," Raine said.

"Like what?" Ember asked.

"Photo albums?" Issy suggested. "Everybody keeps them, and so far we've not found any of Adele's. Seems odd, don't you think? Plus, when Gray and I went to talk to that PI earlier, she said it was photos that led her here to Silver Hollow."

"All right, then." Raine started down the hall toward one of the bedrooms, while Issy and Ember each took the others. None of them, however, found any photo albums or anything else related to Scott's murder trial.

Bella kept squirming inside Issy's hoodie, so finally she pulled the small Pom out and put her on the floor. Instead of staying near Issy, however, the little dog scampered out the door and headed straight for the kitchen. By the time Issy found her, the tiny Pom was flopped down at Dex's feet and begging for his attention. Issy tried calling Bella back as discreetly as she could, but her familiar refused to budge. Just sat there panting and staring up adoringly at Dex. Every so often, Bella would shoot Issy approving looks in between. Seemed her dog had as bad of a crush for Dex as Issy did.

Spectacular. Shaking her head, Issy caught Dex's gaze briefly across the expanse of the open kitchen and hall before ducking back inside the relative safety of the bedroom. The fizzy tingle that had started inside her during their kiss outside now bubbled through her bloodstream, making her both giddy and anxious. She leaned back against the wall and closed her eyes, taking a deep, calming breath.

"Find anything, cuz?" Raine asked, sticking her head around the door. "You okay?"

"I'm fine." Issy forced a bright smile. "Nothing in here. How about you?"

"Nope. Nothing for me either." There was a knowing glint in Raine's eye that made Issy wary as they joined Ember out in the hall then made their way back to the living room, where the guys were now waiting. Dex had taken a seat in one of Adele's old armchairs, and Bella had made herself right at home in his lap while he scratched her behind the ears and smiled.

Lucky dog.

Issy shook her head and took a seat on the arm of the sofa beside her cousins. "Did you tell Dex about the PI, Gray?"

"I didn't have to." Gray leaned over so Cosmo could climb off his shoulder and walk the length of the back of the couch. "He said he talked to her too."

"You did?" Issy frowned at Dex. "When?"

"Right before I came here." He stopped petting Bella, which was apparently unacceptable because the little dog batted his hand with her paw to get his attention again. He chuckled and scratched her again. "She didn't have much to tell me. Showed me the file she'd brought with the pictures, said she thought Adele might've had more evidence here at the house. So, I came over to check it out."

"That's what she told us too," Issy said. "But I'm not sure we can trust her."

"Yeah, I got a funny vibe from her too," Dex said. "I need to do more investigating on her."

"I still don't get how Jerry's involved in all this, though," Raine said.

"Linda told us he was studying to be a PI. And DeeDee said earlier at the juice bar he'd worked as a cop for a while in his early years, so maybe he's reopening Scott's old case as a trial run for future work?" Issy said.

"I don't know." Dex put Bella down then rubbed his hand over his face. "The fact the guy disappeared so suddenly doesn't look good for him."

"Oh." Ember smiled. "I tried to get ahold of my friend at the airport to ask about where Jerry went on his vacation, but the guy's not on duty until tomorrow.

He's supposed to call me first thing in the morning, so I'll let you all know what I find out then."

"I called in a few favors at the Bureau as well, to see if they could trace his ticket numbers and find out his destination, but so far nothing's come through the regular police channels."

"Huh." Issy gave him a small wink. "Guess sometimes it pays to do things unofficially, then."

The heat in his golden-hazel eyes set her belly tingling anew. His full lips quirked into a small half-smile. "Yeah, I guess it does."

"Well, there's nothing more we can do here tonight." Gray held out his arm so Cosmo could climb back onto his shoulder again before he pushed to his feet and yawned. "I'm going home."

Dex sat forward, resting his forearms on his knees, his expression serious. "Wait. I have a question."

The Quinn cousins turned to him.

"If you're all witches, why can't you conjure up the missing stuff from Adele's shelves?"

Gray met Issy's gaze, shocked. "He knows the truth?"

"I knew there was something going on between the two of you!" Ember clapped, her tone triumphant.

"You're not going to haul us in for arrest, are you, Dex?" Raine asked, her expression guarded. "That wouldn't be very nice. Especially since you're dating my cousin now."

"We are not dating," Issy said, the words sounding hollow. She avoided Dex's gaze, though she could feel the weight of his stare. Heat prickled her cheeks as she sought the right words to explain what had happened. "After what he'd seen at Enid's, he was bound to figure it out sooner or later. Especially after Luigi couldn't erase his memory like the first time."

"Wait. What first time?" Dex scowled. "Somebody erased my memory?"

Issy ignored his question and spoke to her cousins instead. "Don't worry. He's promised not to turn us in. He's on our side."

"Is he now?" Gray said, sounding unconvinced.

"I am." Dex looked up and met Gray's gaze. After a few minutes, a silent understanding seemed to pass between the two men. They each gave a curt nod, and Gray sat back down. Dex tried again. "First, tell me who erased my memory and why. And second, explain to me why you guys can't just make this stuff appear. I want to understand."

"It doesn't work that way," Gray said. "Though life would be a lot easier if things worked like they did on *Bewitched*. And your memory was cleaned after the Louella Drummond case by order of our local Witch

Committee. They couldn't risk having a human running around, especially one who worked for the FBPI, after having seen all that magic out in the woods that night."

"I don't remember any of that," Dex said, obviously confused.

"Exactly." Gray grinned.

"I wish things were as easy as *Bewitched*." Raine laughed. "I'd love to be able to conjure myself a new wardrobe whenever I wanted one."

"Or snap my fingers and transport myself to Paris for the day," Ember said, snuggling her kittens. "We'd love to see the Eiffel Tower again."

"Honestly, Dex, your original question would take far longer than one night to answer," Issy said. "Suffice it to say, magic isn't about making things appear and disappear so much as it is about controlling the energy around us and using that energy to manifest what's already there. And intention. Always intention."

"Huh. Yeah, that sort of makes sense, I guess." Dex looked thoughtful. "We'll have to discuss it more someday, though, when we have the time."

Hope flared anew inside Issy that maybe, just maybe, things between her and Dex might work out after all. He'd not balked at her explanation of magic. In fact, if his statement was any indication, he seemed more intrigued than ever. And the promise of them talking more in the future was a bonus, especially if that talking led to more kissing, like it had tonight.

"Hey, Dex," Raine said, her grin devilish. "I just got a new shipment of Chinese Lantern plants in yesterday at the greenhouse. Don't bearded dragons love those as treats?"

"I'm not sure, to be honest." He glanced at Issy, who nodded. "I guess they do."

"Perfect." Raine stood. "The company sent way more than I ordered, so I have extras. I'll drop some off by your house tomorrow."

"Yes!" Ember pushed to her feet as well. "And I made a special fruit concoction that's safe for bearded dragons to eat. I'm sure little Gordon would love it. I'll bring some over along with Raine." She smiled serenely then winked at Issy. "You might as well come along. Say around eleven? That way our assistants can cover the lunch crowd?"

"Oh, I don't know." Issy glanced at Dex uncertainly. Things seemed to be going well between them tonight, and she didn't want to press her luck too far, plus she got the distinct impression her cousins were up to something. "I'm sure Dex is busy tomorrow and—"

"Actually," Dex said, standing and pulling out his phone, his smile amused. "I will be home tomorrow morning. The cable guy is coming to fix something. I'd love to show off my new bungalow to someone other than Gordon." He jotted down his address then handed it to Issy, along with a key to Adele's house.

She grabbed the paper with his address, but he pulled back the key before she could grab it. Issy gave him a confused look, but he just grinned. "On second thought, I'll keep the key. You guys don't need this, right?" He headed for the door, pausing on the threshold. "Just use your magical abilities to lock up before you leave, okay?"

Chapter Fifteen

"Hey, cuz." Raine bustled into Enchanted Pets the next morning, her arms loaded down with Chinese Lantern plants. "Sorry to back out on you at the last minute, but I've got a whole batch of my prized orchids wilting, and I don't have anyone to tend to them." She plopped the pots down on Issy's counter then brushed the dirt off her hands. "Sorry I can't go to Dex's with you."

"Darn." Issy frowned. "Hope your plants get better soon."

Raine waved on her way out the door.

Issy grabbed an empty cardboard box from the back room and set the plants inside then snatched her bag from beneath the counter and fished out her keys. "Hannah? I'm going to load these into Brown Betty. When Ember gets here, can you send her down to my truck? We'll leave from there."

"Sure thing, boss," Hannah said, waving. "Have a good time."

"See you in an hour or so." Issy headed outside, Bella trotting along on her leash. The sun was out, and the day felt warmer than usual. She walked the half a block to her old pickup and balanced the box on one hip while she unlocked the passenger side door then bent inside the truck to settle the box in the small space behind the seats. Nervous excitement fizzed in her stomach, and she couldn't seem to keep the silly grin off her face. Truth was, she hadn't been able to stop thinking about Dex and the latest kiss they'd shared. Seemed each time they were together, the invisible cord between them grew stronger. And now, with him all but coming out and saying he accepted her, magic and all...

Well, Issy felt more hopeful about a possible relationship between them than she had in a long, long time. Now, if Ember would just get a move on, they could head over to Dex's bungalow before his cable guy finished for the morning.

"There you are." Ember rushed down the sidewalk, a small white shopping bag with the Divine Cravings logo embellished on the side in her hand. "I'm really sorry, Issy, but I'm afraid I can't make it today either. Got a big order for a last-minute dinner party tonight and I've got a ton of desserts to make this morning." She held out the bag to Issy. "Here's the lizard treats. Be sure to give him a scratch under the chin for me."

Ember winked, and Issy got the distinct impression she'd just been set up. Still, she asked, "Gordon, you mean?"

"Sure. Him too." Ember slowly backed away. "Have fun!"

Issy shook her head and secured Bella onto the passenger seat before walking around to get in her truck. She'd been nervous enough seeing Dex again with her cousins along. Now, she'd be seeing him again all alone. Her chest squeezed with apprehension. Maybe he'd changed his mind. Maybe he'd decided being with a paranormal was too much bother. Maybe he'd regretted kissing her last night.

She took a deep breath and checked for oncoming traffic before pulling out into the lane and driving the few short blocks from downtown Silver Hollow to the quiet residential neighborhood where Dex had rented his house.

After parking in front of his cute white-and-green bungalow, she got out and walked around the truck to let Bella out. She reached in for Raine's box of plants then grabbed Ember's bag of treats before closing the door with her butt. Swallowing hard against the constriction in her throat, she walked up his front sidewalk to the porch and rang the doorbell with her elbow while Bella yipped beside her, a happy litany of telepathic thoughts bombarding Issy's brain, this time in full sentences at least.

I like it here, Mommy! Lots of interesting smells here, Mommy!

Can we go inside, Mommy?

Dex answered the door, his smile warming her from head to toe.

"Good morning!" He took the box from her arms. "You look great, Issy."

Heat prickled her cheeks as she ran her hand down the front of her black cardigan and slacks. She'd decided to wear something other than her usual jeans and T-shirt today, knowing she'd be coming to see him. The fact he'd noticed—and appreciated her appearance, if the sparkle in his hazel eyes was any indication—made her feel special. She wasn't used to anyone, especially a man she was interested in, taking any notice of how she looked.

"Come on in." Dex waved her inside his home. "The cable guy is still here working in the den, so please excuse the mess."

"Thank you." She passed by him and picked up Bella, catching a whiff of his sandalwood cologne as she stepped into his open-floor-plan living room. Her heels clacked on the gleaming hardwood floors, and the overstuffed furniture and warm paint tones made the giant space feel homey and comfortable. She stood there for a minute, just gazing around, before remembering what was in her hand. "Oh, here. The treats Ember made for Gordon."

He took the bag and set it on the counter beside the box of plants. "Thanks. Where are your cousins? I thought they were coming too."

"They couldn't make it. Sorry. Things at work."

"Ah." One side of his full lips quirked up into a small smile as he took a step toward her. "Guess that means it's just you and me this morning, then, huh?"

"Yeah." Issy stared at the toes of her black pumps, tucking a stray strawberry-blond curl behind her ear with a shaking hand, suddenly shy. "I guess so."

"You can put the dog down, if you want."

"Great." Issy unclipped Bella's leash and set her on the floor. The small Pom's nails scrabbled against the polished floor as she ran over to Gordon's vivarium in the corner of the living room. The little lizard raised his front foot in a wave, and Issy smiled. "How's my little green buddy doing?"

"He's great." Dex reached past her to pull out one of Ember's treats, and Issy did her best to suppress a shudder at his nearness. Together, they walked over to the bearded dragon's enclosure. "Want to try one of these, buddy?"

Issy giggled as Gordon snatched the treat from Dex and gobbled it up like it was going out of style. "He seems to like those."

"Yes, he does." Dex stood close enough that his shoulder brushed against hers.

"So." Dex rocked back on his heels. "We're alone, then."

She caught his eye and blinked. "We are."

Bella yipped as if in protest, and Gordon waved once more.

"Okay." Issy grinned. "Maybe not all alone."

"No. Not all alone." He reached out and hooked his finger beneath Issy's chin. "I missed you."

"You just saw me last night." Her words husked out of her suddenly dry throat.

"I know." His warm breath ghosted over her skin as his soft lips met hers in a featherlight kiss. Those same sparks, brilliant and incandescent, danced between them like fireflies, and she sighed, inching closer to him, her hand resting on Dex's chest, right over his pounding heart. Issy's own pulse thundered in her ears. Dex slipped his arms around her waist to pull her even closer, and she realized the world could stop turning right here and now and she'd die a happy woman.

"All right, sir." The cable guy walked into the living room and set his toolkit down on the hardwood floor with a clatter. Issy jumped away from Dex before he could catch her. "I'll need your signature here on the dotted line, then I'll be out of your hair." The cable guy looked up from his clipboard and glanced from Dex to Issy then back again. "Hope I wasn't interrupting anything."

Issy shook her head and moved to the far side of the living room, not trusting her voice to speak, while Dex took care of business with the cable guy. By the time the repairman left, she'd almost gotten her rapid breath under control. Almost.

Dex closed the door then ran a hand through his dark hair, dots of crimson lining his high cheekbones. If Issy didn't know better, she'd think he was as affected as she was by their brief kiss. He took a deep breath then looked at her again, those sparks flaring brightly between them. Dex headed over to where she stood by the window, his expression intent. "Issy, I think we…"

Frowning, Dex stopped several feet away from her and pulled out his phone. "Sorry. Hang on, I need to take this."

She stared at his retreating back as he headed toward the kitchen area. Knees still a bit wobbly, Issy took a seat on the sofa in the living room and reached down to scratch Bella behind the ears.

Do you like him, Mommy? I like him a lot, Mommy! Can we stay here, Mommy?

"Sorry about that." Dex returned a few moments later. He shut off his phone and shoved the device back in his pocket. "Let me show you around the place."

"Sure. Great." Issy stood, Bella in her arms, and followed him down a short hallway. "This is a nice home."

"Thanks." He glanced back at her over his shoulder, and her heart stumbled. "I haven't been here long enough to do much with it yet."

"You should hang up some pictures. Maybe get some curtains. Personalize it a bit more." She followed him into an empty guest bedroom. "Make it feel more like a home. There's a nice shop in the next town over that specializes in home décor. Last time I was there they had these mission-style lamps that would work perfectly in your living room."

"Hmm." He showed her two more bedrooms and a guest bathroom before walking her back into the living room again. "Well, that's it."

"Very nice. And a great neighborhood too. Lots of families and kids."

"Yeah, I like it here so far."

They both looked anywhere but at each other as awkwardness descended again.

"Can I get you something to drink?" he asked, heading for the kitchen.

Issy trailed behind, stopping to lean against the granite-topped breakfast bar. "No, I'm good, thanks."

He opened the fridge and pulled out a bottled water then leaned his hips back against the counter. "I was actually thinking about calling my landlord and seeing if I could get out of my lease."

"Really?" Issy's heart tumbled to her toes once more. Just when she thought they might have a chance together, he was leaving again. "That's too..."

The sheriff's car pulled into the driveway, capturing their attention and interrupting her words. DeeDee hopped out and jogged up the walkway. Dex met her at the front door.

"DeeDee, what are you doing here?"

She stepped inside, her eyes darting from Issy to Dex. Her brow quirked up, and she held a pile of papers out. "New information on the case. I thought you might want to see it right away. I knew you were at home with the cable guy, and you didn't answer your phone..."

"Umm, I shut it off." Dex reached out for the papers.

Issy glanced at the stack as DeeDee handed them off. The information must have been important if she'd taken the time to drive it over. Issy's heart skipped when she saw a name on the top. Linda Brewer. Was it a background check? A criminal record? She was only able to see one other thing before Dex grabbed the papers and hid them from view. Linda Brewer lived in Lowell, Massachusetts—the same town Sarah Landers had been from.

"I hope I didn't interrupt anything." DeeDee smirked.

Issy glanced at Dex, heat burning her cheeks. "Oh no. I was just leaving."

Issy reluctantly picked up Bella. Even though Dex's kiss still had her all twisted up, she had more important things on her mind now. She needed to convey this new information to her cousins right away. Besides, Dex was breaking his lease. He was leaving town. So what was the point in carrying on with him, anyway?

"See you later." She tossed the words casually over her shoulder as she skipped out the door and all but ran to Brown Betty.

Chapter Sixteen

Issy texted her cousins for an emergency meeting, and they decided to convene at Raine's shop. Inside, the place was lush with tropical plants. The humidity was stifling, and Issy shrugged out of her jacket, tossing it behind the counter. It was as if she'd been transported to a tropical island, right down to the tinkling sound of a waterfall in the back and the scent of gardenias that hung like a cloud in the air.

"So, what's up?" Gray leaned against the counter next to Mortimer, who angled his toothy petals toward them as if listening in on the conversation. Issy didn't doubt that he was listening. Raine often left Morty at suspects' homes or places of business to eavesdrop on conversations. They had a special telepathic link, and he could transmit images or ideas that only Raine could interpret. Sometimes he'd wilt or perk up depending on what he'd overheard.

"I was just at Dex's," Issy started.

"We don't really want to know the details of your sex life." Raine wiggled her eyebrows.

Issy's heart dropped. Before she'd left Dex's, he'd told her he was getting out of his lease. At least he'd been honest and let her know that anything with him would be short-lived. When he'd taken the keys and told her to lock up with magic the night before, she'd taken it as an acceptance of her magic. But he must have changed his mind, and now he was leaving town, dashing her hopes that they could be one of the rare witch-human relationships that worked out. But she didn't want her cousins to know how devastated that made her, so she made a playful face at Raine. "Not that. While I was there, DeeDee came by with important information. A sheet on Linda Brewer, and guess where Linda Brewer is from?"

"Where?"

"Lowell, Massachusetts. The same exact place Sarah Landers was from."

"That is interesting. Do you think Linda was somehow mixed up in this case ten years ago? Is that really why she's here?" Ember played with the stunning pink-and-green striped leaves of a watermelon coleus plant.

"It's possible," Issy said. "She was about the same age as Scott. She could have been at that spring break. She could have known Sarah Landers."

"But if she knew Sarah and she knew something about the murder, why wouldn't she have come forward back then?" Gray asked.

"She wouldn't come forward if she was the killer or was protecting the killer," Raine suggested.

"But when we visited her in the motel, she had all the case files. She was clearly investigating it, and she wouldn't need to do that if she was the killer, right?" Gray said.

"She *looked* like she was investigating it," Issy corrected. "But what if she was really here trying to cover things up? She might have gotten new information just like she said. If she was the killer, it makes sense that she'd try to keep track of the case. The spell Raine put on the orchid was just a relaxing spell, not a truth spell. Even though she gave up a lot of information, she could have been tweaking it to make it look like she was investigating when in fact she had come here to cover things up."

"So then where does Jerry fit in?" Ember asked.

"He's easily manipulated, and he was around back then. Maybe he knows more than he thinks. She might be trying to figure out what he knows... and if he knew too much, she might have gotten rid of him too. That could be why his shop is closed."

"And she could have lied about him being on vacation to throw us off track. That vacation seems awfully sudden to me, and he didn't mention anything about that when we talked to him the other day," Issy said.

Raine pressed her lips together and stroked the back of one of Morty's glossy leaves. "I don't like the way this is shaping up. Something isn't right here."

"I agree," Issy said. "Looks like we need to beef up that spell on your pansy orchid and pay Linda Brewer another visit."

Chapter Seventeen

Fifteen minutes later Issy was inside Brown Betty rushing toward the Route Nine Motel. Raine was seated beside her with a quivering pansy orchid balanced on her lap.

"This thing is juiced up with the super truth serum. There's no way Linda is going to lie to us while Prudence is there."

"Prudence?" Issy glanced at Raine.

"The plant."

Issy swerved hard right to avoid a big fat toad in the middle of the road. "I hope we get some answers. I'm getting sick of these toads everywhere. You'd think the cold would drive them underground."

"I agree. Five families of toads have taken refuge inside my Easter lilies in the back of the shop. These things have to go. We need to solve this case soon."

Issy pulled into a parking spot near Room 127. They hopped out of the car and headed toward Linda's room.

Raine slowed as they approached the door. "Uh-oh. This doesn't look good." She pointed at the slight gap in the door which indicated it wasn't closed all the way.

"Maybe she forgot to close it." Issy tapped her knuckles on the door. "Linda, it's Issy Quinn. I came back with the plant like I said I would."

No answer.

Issy and Raine exchanged a glance.

"Linda?" Issy yelled louder.

Still nothing.

"Maybe she's in the shower?" Raine ventured.

"With the door ajar?" Issy pushed down the panic that rose in her chest and nudged the door open slowly.

The room was a mess. Papers strewn everywhere, the maple floor lamp lying on the gold shag carpet, its shade cock-eyed. But the worst part was on the floor next to the bed. Linda Brewer's bloody body.

Smash!

Issy whirled around to see Raine standing openmouthed in the doorway, the plant smashed at her feet.

"Prudence!" Raine threw herself on the ground, scooping the dirt into a pile and trying to put the pieces of the smashed pot back together to stuff the plant back in. Issy had other priorities. She ran into the motel room and crouched beside Linda. She could still be alive and need her help. But Linda's glazed eyes staring up at the ceiling told her otherwise. She pressed her fingertips to her neck anyway.

No pulse.

"Is she dead?" Raine stood just outside the door, the pieced-together broken pot encircled in her arms, plant quivering out of the top.

Issy backed carefully out of the room, her stomach churning. "I'm afraid so." She stumbled a few feet down the sidewalk, pulled out her phone, and called the police.

***

Dex careened into the Route Nine Motel parking lot, his heart twisting at the sight of Issy sitting on the curb, her knees pulled up to her chest, her face ashen. Relief mixed with self-recrimination flooded through him. When the call had come in and DeeDee had said there was a murder and Issy was here, he'd gone half-mad with worry. Now he was relieved to see she was okay. But his relief was tempered with the sinking sensation of failure. Once again, he hadn't been able to protect her.

Then again, the woman was a murder-magnet. How could he possibly protect her all the time? He couldn't. He didn't know if he could handle Issy's frequent bouts with danger, especially when he couldn't be around to keep her safe all the time. Would she even want him if he couldn't? Maybe things wouldn't work out between them the way he was hoping after all.

When she'd visited his bungalow earlier that day, it had felt good to have her in his home. He'd finally thought maybe he was getting somewhere with her, getting her to open her heart to him a bit more. Heck, she'd even given him some decorating advice on that quick tour of his place. He'd even been considering inviting her over again to help him spruce up the bungalow. But now…

He slammed the car into park, and Issy stood, a bit wobbly on her feet.

He should have tended to the crime scene first, but the hell with it. He rushed to her side.

"Are you okay?" He wrapped his arms around her. She melted into him, as if she belonged there, making his doubts about their budding relationship vanish at least temporarily. He pushed her to arm's length, just to make sure she wasn't hurt.

"I'm fine," she said.

"Me too." Raine waved from beside Issy. Had she been there the whole time? Dex had only had eyes for Issy.

He took a deep breath and stepped away. "What happened?"

"We came to talk to Linda and found her in there." Issy nodded toward the motel room. "Dead."

DeeDee squealed to a stop a few parking spots away from Dex and walked over to join them. Refocusing his attention on work, Dex reluctantly left Issy and led the way into the motel room. More squad cars arrived, and soon clusters of cops and detectives stood around the scene, talking or keeping away rubberneckers.

Someone set up police lights, and soon the gruesome scene was lit up like a Broadway play. Linda Brewer was sprawled on the floor beside the bed, a growing crimson stain spreading across the front of her shirt from her bullet wound. Glass littered the floor where the thief had smashed the mirror above the dresser. The victim's belongings were strewn all over the place. The coppery smell of death mixed with mildew.

"Did anyone see what happened?" Dex asked.

"They're still rounding up witnesses." DeeDee scanned the area, frowning. "From the way they trashed this place, though, I'd say whoever killed her was definitely looking for something."

"Adele's place was trashed too." Dex narrowed his gaze. "Maybe whoever killed Adele didn't find what they were looking for at her place and came here instead."

"Or maybe Linda stumbled onto something she shouldn't have," Issy said, venturing into the room and straight to Dex's side. "Who would do such an awful thing?"

DeeDee leaned in closer and whispered, "You were both here the other day. Do either of you notice anything missing? Something that might give us a lead?"

Dex looked around, but with all the crap everywhere, it was hard to tell.

Issy walked over to the dresser then to the bathroom and finally to the closet before she returned to Dex's side. "The file she had is gone. When Gray and I came here, she showed us the folder she'd been gathering on the murder. She said she was getting closer to proving Scott was innocent once and for all. She said she came here to talk to Jerry to get the whole picture of what Scott was like before he went on that vacation to Florida, but I think she was lying about something. I don't see the folder anywhere around here now."

"Makes sense the killer would take it," Dex agreed. "If there was something incriminating in those files, they'd want that information hidden. But what was she hiding? I felt like she wasn't being straight with me either."

"The only thing I could think of is that she was involved in the murder," Issy said.

DeeDee paused from her task and squinted up at Issy. "I don't think so. Not after what the background check revealed."

"What was that?" Linda must have known Sarah, but what else had been on that paper that would make DeeDee so sure that she wasn't her killer?

"Linda Brewer was Sarah Landers's sister."

Issy stared at DeeDee. "So that's why she's from the same town."

DeeDee narrowed her gaze. "How'd you know that?"

"Umm... I did some research. No wonder she was out here looking for the killer. That's why she'd followed the case all these years. I guess she was telling the truth. She really did find new evidence."

"Yeah, too bad the killer must have figured that out," Dex said.

"But who would have known that she had the new evidence?" Issy asked.

"Good question. We might find the answer in the missing paperwork," Dex said.

"Right, well, this kind of speculation is baseless. We need facts." DeeDee sighed. "Too bad the killer could've done anything with that paperwork by now. That doesn't leave us much to go on here."

"Wait." Issy leaned closer to the bed, her gaze narrowed on Linda's corpse. "There's something in her hand."

DeeDee moved in as well and squinted. "You're right."

Dex pulled Issy close to his side once more. Part of him wanted to carry her out of here and shield her from all this carnage, to keep her safe and secure and near him forever. The other part of him was duty bound to stand guard over the victim and make sure justice was done.

If the good deputy noticed him holding Issy's hand, she didn't say a word. DeeDee hailed over one of the crime-scene techs and got a pair of gloves to remove the evidence from Linda's hand to prevent contamination. Nose wrinkled, she held up the crinkled object. "Looks like a photograph."

Issy clutched Dex's forearm tightly. Even under the current circumstances, awareness zinged over his skin from their point of contact. "I've seen that picture before," Issy said. "When Gray and I were here, Linda showed us that one. It's of the plastic visitor's badge Jerry gave Scott at the paper mill before he left on his Florida trip."

"What do you think this means?" DeeDee asked.

"Could be Jerry cooperating with Linda had less to do with him studying to be a PI and more so he could keep an eye on her and see exactly what kind of evidence she'd uncovered." Dex scowled. "Maybe Linda's trying to tell us the identity of her murderer."

"Jerry?" DeeDee said.

"Jerry can't be the killer. He's out of town on vacation, remember?" Issy straightened. "Or maybe Jerry just tried to make it look like he was out of town so he'd have an alibi."

Dex remembered how squirrelly the guy had acted at his body shop the other day and squeezed Issy's fingers reassuringly. If Dex hadn't shown up when he did, there was no telling what Jerry might've done to Issy. Which put the guy at the top spot on Dex's most wanted list.

"Well, either way"—DeeDee slipped the tattered photo into an evidence bag held by one of the techs then snapped off her gloves—"I'd say we need to locate Jerry Blaisdale and bring him in for questioning."

Chapter Eighteen

"Look who decided to join us." Issy held her hand over her eyes to block out the midafternoon sun. She and her cousins had called another emergency meeting at The Main Squeeze after what had happened to Linda Brewer that morning. "Had some cancelations this afternoon, Gray?"

"No." He took a seat at their table and leaned back slightly to allow Cosmo to step off onto his chair. "Just a lighter schedule than normal today. So, catch me up on what I've missed."

"Well, I was just telling them what I found out from my friend at the airport," Ember said. "My friend is pretty sure Jerry got on that plane—or at least someone who looked exactly like him did."

"How are they so sure?" Issy asked then took a sip of her Pumpkin Perfection spiced juice blend. Owing to the cooler weather, the owner of the juice bar, Karen Dixon, had changed up her menu and was trying out some new seasonal promotions. The flavors of cinnamon and cloves filled her mouth and tickled her nose.

"Security footage at boarding," Ember said.

"That's what I'm saying." Raine wrinkled her nose at the green concoction in her cup—a Green Goblin Surprise, according to the menu board nearby. "With all the security checks these days, it would be hard to impersonate someone else. Not to mention the steep fines and possible jail time if you got caught. Seems like an awful lot of trouble and risk for Jerry to have someone impersonate him."

"I'll have my friend double-check the tapes again to be sure," Ember said, kissing the top of Endora's furry black head. Then she bent to do the same to Bellatrix's white coat, stopping and squinting at the next table over. "Hey, isn't that the guy DeeDee was talking about the other day? The movie producer?"

Gray leaned slightly to peer past Issy. "Looks like him, yeah. Must be one of his out-of-town blond babes sitting with him. I've not seen her in my shop."

Issy glanced over as discreetly as she could then turned back to her cousins, a familiar tingle starting deep inside her. "He's paranormal. They're drinking Pomegranate Passions too. And you know the effect those things have on us."

"Aw, man." Raine shook her head and pushed her cup away, grimacing with distaste. "I was trying to ignore that tingle, for DeeDee's sake. The last thing she needs right now is more paranormals to look after. Especially now that the poor thing is being forced into a marriage with a virtual stranger. Sounds crazy to me."

"Not so crazy." Ember rubbed her chin on the top of Bellatrix's head. "Silver Hollow is a mecca for our kind, so I'm betting it's no coincidence: Not with the kind of movies DeeDee said he makes. Maybe he's looking to find some fresh talent for his next picture."

"Whatever he's doing here, he better watch himself." Gray cocked his head toward the interior of the juice bar and the Hagrid-on-acid-looking guy glaring out the front window. "Looks like Luigi's got Mr. Hollywood on his radar already."

Glancing inside, Issy spotted Luigi behind the counter as usual, selling slices of his pizza. While he was waiting on customers, he was giving the town's newest arrival some seriously skeptical side-eye.

She shook her head and gazed out toward the sidewalk again, only to see Brimstone trotting by. He gave the movie producer a feline stare of disapproval. Seems no one wanted the new filmmaker to come to Silver Hollow.

"So what else do we know about Jerry?" Gray asked, sipping his Saffron Sunrise. "That's too bad about what happened to Linda Brewer, by the way. I guess our previous assumption that she might be the killer was wrong."

Issy, Ember, and Raine exchanged a glance. "How'd you hear about that already? I just left the scene right before I came here and told Ember and Raine before you arrived."

"Myra Bell was in to get her hair done."

Issy nodded. Myra was the receptionist for the sheriff's department and could be fairly loose-lipped with the intel when it suited her purposes. Then again, with the miracles of beauty worked in Gray's enchanted salon, every woman was susceptible to persuasion. It was one of the things that made Sheer Magic so successful. Well, that and the fact Gray looked like he walked right off the pages of some male fashion magazine, with his long dark hair and piercing blue eyes. All the ladies went gaga for him, including Myra, it seemed.

Exhaling slowly, Issy forced her mind back to the task at hand. Now they had two murders to solve. She suppressed a shudder as images of Linda Brewer, lying facedown on the blood-soaked bed, flooded her thoughts. "Dex wondered if Jerry working with Linda Brewer had less to do with him studying to be a PI and more to do with him being involved in that murder ten years ago."

"Interesting theory." Raine rubbed Mortimer's leaves gently, her gaze narrowed. "Was Jerry down in Florida during spring break then?"

"That would be odd," Ember said. "He would've been a lot older than the college kids."

Gray shrugged. "Wouldn't be the first time some older guy liked dating younger girls."

"Ew." Issy shuddered anew. "What if he's some kind of paranormal serial killer? Icky."

"Well." Raine stood and tossed her barely touched drink into a nearby trash can then tucked Morty's pot under her arm. "I need to get back to my greenhouse. We should probably go talk to someone at Holland Mills and find out if Jerry took time off during spring break ten years ago."

"Good idea." Ember settled Endora and Bellatrix in their basket then pushed to her feet as well. "I can whip up a batch of chocolates infused with a loose-tongue charm for my friend Gladys who works in the office over there. The dear woman has to be pushing ninety by now."

"If anyone would know, it would be her." Gray settled back while Cosmo danced and cawed on the back of the chair. "She's worked for the Hollands forever."

"At least fifty years," Ember said, waving as she followed Raine down the sidewalk. "Issy, text me when you're ready to head over and I'll go with you."

"Will do." Issy kissed the top of Bella's head then put her down and wrapped the little dog's pink-and-rhinestone leash around her hand. "I need to get back to Enchanted Pets. Hannah will be wondering where I am. Are you staying?"

"I don't have another client for an hour, so I figured I'd soak up some sun and enjoy my rare free time." Gray winked. "Have fun at the paper mill later."

"Thanks." Issy gave Cosmo a goodbye scratch on the head then led Bella back toward the pet store. "I'll let you know what we find out."

Chapter Nineteen

"That's confirmed?" Dex asked as he waited on the corner for the light to change. It seemed weird to be walking downtown in Silver Hollow without his best bud Gordon perched on his shoulder, but he hadn't had a chance to stop at home after he'd left the crime scene at the motel. "Jerry Blaisdale was accounted for on that flight yesterday?"

"Yep," DeeDee said through the phone line. "On his way to Bermuda. I also verified he checked into his hotel down there, *and* I found out something interesting from the Route Nine Motel manager."

"What?"

"She said she chased off someone wearing a dark hoodie with a white stripe down one arm a few hours before Linda's body was discovered."

"Scott's girlfriend, Marcy."

"I think so. Motel manager said she had long, scraggly hair. Seems that girl is turning up everywhere, and that's no coincidence. She might have something to do with both deaths, and since Linda is dead and

Jerry is in Bermuda, it's looking like neither of them did, so I say we move Marcy up on the suspect list."

"I don't know." Dex followed the small crowd of locals and tourists across the street. He'd parked his Buick about half a block away, thinking some fresh air and exercise might help him forget the blood and gore he'd witnessed earlier. Balancing his cell phone between his shoulder and jaw, he searched his pockets for paper and a pen. "Why would she kill Adele?"

"Maybe she was upset after Scott died and wanted some mementos. She probably knew about the box Adele kept, maybe she went there to get it and Adele wouldn't give it to her so she killed her. It's possible Adele's death had nothing to do with the murder ten years ago."

"I agree it's a lead we should follow. It makes sense. Marcy might have killed Adele by mistake when they were arguing and run off into the woods. That's why the neighbor didn't see her. If she ran in the same direction as the other night, she wouldn't have gone past the neighbor's house. And then she might have come back and broken in to get the box the other night."

"Exactly."

"But something still doesn't seem quite right about this whole thing. I want to be thorough. I'd like to question Jerry myself. Do you have his cell number?"

DeeDee rattled off the digits, and Dex scribbled them down.

"Okay, thanks, Deputy." He shoved the number and his pen back into his pants pocket. "Not that I don't think you and Owen did a thorough job. I just want to confirm this isn't some elaborate ruse he's cooked up to throw us off the trail."

After hanging up with DeeDee, Dex punched in the numbers for Jerry Blaisdale's phone then stopped near the brick wall of the local bank while the call connected.

"Hello?" Jerry picked up on the third ring, his tone a blend of nerves and confusion. "Who is this?"

"Mr. Blaisdale, this is Agent Dexter Nolan with the FBI office in Silver Hollow. We spoke the other day at your body shop. I'm sorry to bother you on your vacation, but I've got some additional questions I need to ask you."

"I've already told you everything I know about Adele Brundage," Jerry said.

"This isn't about Adele, I'm afraid." Dex exhaled slowly. "Linda Brewer was found dead in her motel room today, the victim of an apparent robbery gone wrong."

"Linda's been… Oh crap. I-I don't know anything about that either," Jerry said, his words rushed. "I swear. I wasn't even in town. My flight left early yesterday morning."

"Kind of hard to afford a trip to Bermuda on a mechanic's salary, isn't it, Jerry?" Dex frowned, playing his hunches.

"I won the trip. Got it free from my old employer. They're good to those that worked for them, you know? Even though I parted ways with them years ago, they still put my name in for that monthly prize." He gave a nervous chuckle. "This is my second time winning too, so I guess I'm doubly lucky with them. All I can say is that paper mill really knows how to treat their own."

"Unfortunately, Mr. Blaisdale, I'm going to need more than your word that you're actually in Bermuda right now." Was Jerry lying about the paper mill sending him on vacation so he could have the perfect alibi?

"Here." The muffled sounds of Jerry fumbling with his phone echoed through the line. "I'll put you on FaceTime."

Dex clicked the green camera button on his own phone and up popped Jerry's face, the hotel room, and white-sand Bermuda beaches and ocean, visible through the windows behind him. It must've been windy because the palm trees outside were blowing, their fronds whistling and smacking against the glass doors. From somewhere in the distance a loud bang reverberated, and Jerry ducked then scrambled over to the balcony. Through the video feed, Dex could see a scooter down on the street, the tire blown out.

"See, Agent Nolan?" Jerry gave him a wobbly smile. "I'm right here, just like I said."

Dex sighed. Couldn't argue with the reality staring him in the face. Regardless of his instincts telling him otherwise, Jerry Blaisdale probably didn't kill Linda. He was definitely in Bermuda now, and unless he'd somehow finagled the flight times, he'd been there since before her death.

"What was your relationship with Linda Brewer?" Dex asked.

"Relationship? We didn't have one. She was investigating an old case and needed my help." His tone reflected a smudge of pride. "I'm studying for my private investigator's license, you know."

"I know," Dex said. "And I know she was investigating the Sarah Landers case. But what I don't know is what your involvement in *that* case is."

"Involvement?" Jerry's voice quivered, and Dex heard a tire blow out on Jerry's end. "I didn't have one.

I mean I knew the killer, Scott. But I wasn't involved in the murder or anything."

"Really? That case happened a decade ago. Didn't you think it was kind of odd that she was investigating it now?"

"No. I didn't think of it," Jerry said. "I thought it would be a good way to hone my skills for my new PI business. Didn't really care much if it was an old case or not. I guess maybe I should have asked?"

"Maybe. But it's too late now. Thank you for speaking to me again, Mr. Blaisdale. I'll be in touch."

He finished the call and shoved his phone back into his pocket, rubbing a hand over his face. Jerry had seemed like he was telling the truth, but he also could be tied to all three murders. He needed to check out flights more thoroughly and find out exactly why Linda Brewer had chosen this exact week to come to town.

He wasn't ready to go back to the office, yet he didn't want to go home for lunch and sit alone at his kitchen table either. Dex glanced over and saw The Main Squeeze nearby. He'd heard good things about their juices and the pizza sold inside. Maybe he'd try that today instead.

"Dex?" a voice called.

A guy waved, and it took Dex a minute to squint through the sun to see Issy's cousin Gray seated at one of the outdoor tables, motioning him over. Dex hesitated. He didn't exactly get the impression that Gray liked him, but if he intended to continue to spend time with Issy, he'd have to get on the guy's good side sometime. Besides, some company might do him good right now, after what he'd dealt with this morning, even if the guy was a hairdresser. Dex still wasn't sure what to make of that profession, but hey. Company was company.

"Good to see you again," Dex said, walking up and shaking Gray's hand. "Let me run inside and grab a slice and a drink and I'll be right back. You want anything?"

"No, I'm good, thanks." Gray sat back to coo to his pet bird while Dex headed inside the juice bar. The interior was modern yet held onto its original roots by keeping many of the exposed beams and brick and the industrial pipes overhead. He got two slices of deluxe pizza from that huge bearded guy, Luigi, then grabbed a Saffron Sunrise before heading back outside to join Gray at his table. The sun was shining, and it was warmer than usual, making Dex glad he had an opportunity to enjoy the outdoors while he still could.

"How's your day going?" Dex asked as he took a seat. "No clients in the salon today?"

"My schedule's lighter than usual." Gray grinned then fed his bird a slice of orange from his drink. "Figured I'd take advantage of the sunshine."

"I was thinking the same thing," Dex said, before devouring a large bite of his pizza. The tomato sauce was amazing—slightly sweet with a hint of spice and garlic—and the salty sausage all but melted in his mouth. He could see why people were raving about this stuff all over the area. "Have you talked to Issy today?"

"Yeah, she and my other two cousins were here earlier. They left right before you came." Gray took another sip of his drink. "Too bad about what happened to Linda Brewer."

"Yeah." Dex wiped his mouth with a paper napkin, his spirits sinking slightly. If he'd arrived at the juice bar a little earlier, he might've seen Issy again. Not that they hadn't seen enough of each other today, but it felt like the skies were a little less blue when she wasn't around. The thought both amazed and scared him. Mostly scared him because even though Issy had seemed quite receptive at his bungalow, he'd sensed a change in her at the motel. No doubt she was having second thoughts about what a lousy boyfriend he'd be if he couldn't even protect her from stumbling on a dead body connected with a case he was working.

Might be better not to get in any deeper with the bewitching pet-store owner. Maybe it would be best for both of them if he just moved on. The trouble was, he feared he might have already gotten in too deep where Issy Quinn was concerned.

"Ember said her friend at the airport confirmed Jerry Blaisdale got on a plane yesterday," Gray said, breaking Dex out of his thoughts. "Not sure where to, or even if it was him, though."

"Yeah, it was him." Dex finished off his first slice of pizza. "My sources at the Bureau finally came through. I just talked to DeeDee. And I called Jerry to confirm. He's in Bermuda. He showed me the room and his view on FaceTime and everything."

"Huh." Gray scowled. "Pretty fancy trip for a guy who owns a body shop. I can't even afford that, and I run the most successful salon in the area."

"That's what I thought too." Dex took a large gulp of his juice. The juice was darn good too, the sweetness of the fruit the perfect foil to the savory goodness of the pizza. "I asked him about it, and Jerry said he won the trip from some monthly drawing they have for the employees out at the paper mill. Have you ever heard of the contest?"

"No, but that doesn't mean anything. I don't know many people who work there personally. Ember knows a few. In fact, she and Issy were planning to go out there later today to talk to another friend of Ember's who works there. They think Jerry might be more involved with the murder of Sarah Landers than anyone thought."

"Hmm." Dex started in on his second slice of pizza, swallowing before he continued. "All I know is the guy's alibi checks out for Linda Brewer's murder. He wasn't in town at the time of her death, so it couldn't have been him. Are you sure it's safe for the girls to go out to the mill by themselves today?" Dex frowned. "If Jerry was somehow involved in that case a decade ago, that could be dangerous."

Gray's affable smile dissolved into a hard stare. "Jerry's in Bermuda, and besides, we can take care of ourselves, Agent."

Well, crap. Now he'd gone and offended the guy, and he hadn't meant to. It was just the thought of Issy being at risk and him not being there to help that bugged Dex to no end. He decided to change the subject to smooth things over. He hiked his chin toward the cockatoo currently nuzzling Gray's ear. "Your bird's a nice-looking fellow. Reminds me of that one on TV back in the seventies."

"This is Cosmo." Gray tapped the table, and the bird flew over. With his yellow plume feathers raised cautiously, the cockatoo slowly made his way over to Dex. Slowly, he lifted his hand to run his index finger over the top of the bird's silky head. Before he knew what was happening, Cosmo had climbed up on his forearm then quickly sidestepped his way up to his shoulder, where he preened Dex's hair with his beak. "Friendly, isn't he?"

"He likes you," Gray said, his smile returning. "That's a good sign."

A loud croak sounded, followed by an enormous toad jumping right onto what was left of Dex's pizza. Nose wrinkled, he pushed the food away. "Guess I'm done with that."

"The toads are terrible." Gray shoved another two aside who'd hopped up onto the table. "And they won't be getting better until—" Gray stopped and looked at Dex, only then realizing what he was saying.

"Until what?" Dex asked.

"Oh," Gray said, looking away. "Until their mating season is over. That's why they're so plentiful right now. They come out for a few weeks like this, but they'll be gone soon."

The slight rise in the guy's tone told Dex that story wasn't entirely true, but he had too many other things on his mind right now to worry about the local toad population. Dex just shrugged and chuckled again as Cosmo tickled his ear.

"You should cut the sides shorter," Gray said.

"Excuse me?"

"Your hair. The next time you get it cut. Tell whoever does it that you want the sides shorter and to leave the top longer."

Dex snorted. "I'll be sure to let my barber know. He just takes the scissors and snip, snip. I'm done."

"Whatever." Gray sniffed then gazed out over the town green. "So, the FBPI, huh? Bet you've got some pretty strong views on magic and witchcraft."

"Not really." He narrowed his gaze on the guy across from him. Gray seemed like a nice enough person, and knowing how close Issy was with her cousins, he was probably just looking out for her since he'd seen her and Dex kissing. It was nice, him being protective of Issy. Dex shrugged. "Live and let live, I say."

Gray looked at him again. "Even after what happened that night at Enid's?"

Cutting to the chase, Dex leaned forward and rested his hands on the wrought iron tabletop. "Listen. I know about the paranormal population here in Silver Hollow. I know you and your cousins are a part of it and there's a lot of magic going on in the area. As long as everyone stays safe and abides by the law, I'm okay with it."

Gray's stern expression wavered, and Dex glimpsed a fleeting loneliness in the guy that matched his own. Hard to believe he'd be lonely when the ladies obviously fawned all over him, but there it was. Not that Dex spent a lot of time thinking about stuff like that, but it did spark his own determination to move things along with Issy.

He still had no idea how he would keep her safe from all these forces he couldn't see and didn't understand, but he'd have to find a way in order for their relationship to deepen. Even if it seemed like Issy was the one protecting him sometimes. That thought didn't sit well with Dex, but the last thing he wanted was to grow old and even more alone. He craved connection and company, craved a tight-knit family and community like the one Issy shared with her cousins. If the sadness in Gray's eyes was any indication, maybe they all just wanted to belong.

Honestly, Dex liked the guy, despite their rocky start and their differences. "Well, if the girls are going over to the mill later, then I guess that leaves the homeless people for me to question. Especially Scott's girlfriend."

"Good luck." Gray tapped the tabletop again, and Cosmo walked back over to him. "Like I said. When we tried to talk to her, Marcy ran away."

"Yeah." Dex shooed the toad off his plate before tossing his trash in the bin next to him. "Well, she was dating Scott. Then she broke into Adele's place looking for who knows what. When DeeDee talked with the front desk manager at the motel Linda was staying at, a woman matching Marcy's description with a striped hoodie was hanging around the motel before Linda was murdered. This girl needs to be questioned, and it needs to happen sooner rather than later."

"Agreed." Gray stood and threw his empty drink cup away. "Hey, whatever happened with the break-in at the funeral home? That whole thing was weird too."

"How'd you know about that?"

Gray shrugged. "News travels fast in the Hollow."

"Another loose end I need to tie up." Dex pushed to his feet as well. "I hate loose ends."

"Me too." Gray grinned. "Unless they're teased and sprayed and arranged just so. See you around, man."

"See ya." Dex raised his hand as Gray walked away then pulled his buzzing phone from his pocket. A new text from his landlord flashed on-screen.

OPEN TO CANCELLING 6 MO TERM

He hadn't expected to change his plans about staying in Silver Hollow so soon after arriving, but sometimes things just don't turn out like you planned.

Chapter Twenty

"Do you have the chocolates?" Issy asked as she and Ember walked up the front steps to the entrance of Holland Mills. The afternoon sun glinted off the large golden letters above the door, and the warm earth-toned brick façade all but screamed wealth and privilege. Issy double-checked her hair in the shiny brass dedication plaque beside the glass front doors, wondering again if she should've changed before coming here.

Ember, of course, looked lovely as always in her dark-brown wool circle skirt and matching russet-colored cashmere sweater. How her cousin managed to look so good and stay so serene while working in a hot kitchen all day, Issy would never know. Even magic had its limits. Heck, most days Issy felt lucky just to stay one step ahead of the constant influx of animals into and out of her busy shop.

"Got the candy right here," Ember said, smoothing a hand down the front of her perfectly pressed skirt. "Ready to go inside? If I remember correctly, Gladys's desk should be straight ahead through the lobby."

Issy nodded, and they proceeded up to the top of the steps, where a uniformed security guard let them into the airy expanse of the lobby atrium. Sunlight filtered through the air, and lush tropical plants of all descriptions from Raine's greenhouse thrived in the temperature-controlled environment. Their heels clacked on the gleaming tile floor as they walked toward a large, modern oak receptionist desk. The woman behind it was small and wrinkled and looked like some fantasy version of everyone's favorite grandmother. Her silver-white hair sparkled in the bright sunshine, and her blue eyes were shining and alert behind her horn-rimmed glasses. Gladys Morestein might be pushing one hundred years old, but her mind and memory were still sharp as tacks.

A large white banner above Gladys's desk proclaimed the hundredth anniversary of Holland Mills, and off to one side were life-sized cardboard cutouts of Troy Holland and Len Childs glad-handing with local civic leaders and charity organizations beneath the headline, "Holland Mills: Giving Back to the Silver Hollow Community."

There were also posters scattered about, showing Troy and Len volunteering in various locations—senior citizen centers and branch campuses of New Hampshire's colleges, where Holland Mills offered scholarships and internships to disadvantaged students.

"My stars!" Gladys said, lowering her glasses down her nose to stare at Issy and Ember over the top. "If it isn't the Quinn girls. Why, it's been at least three years since I've seen you both. To what do I owe this honor, ladies?"

"Hello, Gladys," Ember said, sliding the box of enchanted chocolates discreetly onto the counter. "We were in the area and thought we'd stop by to say hello. I happened to have a batch of these fresh candies in my car and figured I'd share some with you to celebrate your employer's success."

"Yes, Holland Mills does a lot of good around here." Gladys beamed proudly.

"And is good to their employees," Issy said. "You know, giving out vacations and monthly prizes."

Gladys frowned. "Well, I did win a turkey at Thanksgiving last year, but I never got a vacation."

Ember elbowed Issy in the ribs. She got the message. Maybe the vacations didn't extend to receptionists.

"It's just nice to get anything extra, isn't it?" Issy said.

"Oh yes." Gladys nodded. "And what about you, young lady? How are things at Enchanted Pets?"

"Good, thank you, Ms. Morestein." Issy gave the older woman a polite smile.

Gladys harrumphed. "Nonsense. I've known you and your families since you were both in diapers. You call me Gladys."

"Okay, Gladys," Issy said, her smile widening.

"Let me just try one of these chocolates, then," Gladys said, opening the box Ember had set in front of her. "Oh, caramels. These are my favorites."

Issy exchanged a look with Ember as the older lady devoured three of the candies right in a row. Hopefully, they wouldn't cause the same belching problem they had with the spell Ember had used at Enid's a while back. Issy didn't think burping would be tolerated in the pristine confines of the Holland Mills lobby, no matter how philanthropic they pretended to be.

"So, Gladys," Ember said, giving Issy a wink. "We wanted to ask you about a former employee here at the mill. A man by the name of Jerry Blaisdale."

Gladys paused midbite of her fourth caramel and stared at Ember for a moment. Issy's pulse quickened as the seconds seemed to tick by more slowly. Was Gladys on to their little spell? Would she toss them out on the street? Call security? Maybe even the police?

Heat skittered up from beneath the turtleneck collar of Issy's sweater to storm her cheeks. If Gladys called Owen's office, that would mean Dex would find out where they were, since he apparently assisted on all their cases now. She'd die of embarrassment. She'd have to stay clear of him after their kiss this morning. She'd...

"Oh, yes. Jerry. I remember him well. Nice, nice man." Gladys grinned, shoving the rest of the candy in her mouth. "A bit quirky. I remember things would break whenever he was around."

"Yes." Ember nodded and nudged Issy in the side, giving her a some-help-here-would-be-appreciated look. "That's Jerry."

"Gladys, I've heard your memory is exemplary," Issy said, her courage growing as the older lady popped another chocolate out of the box. "Do you happen to recall if he took any time off about ten years ago to go on spring break with a group of college kids?"

"Hmm." Gladys frowned, seeming to consider this deeply. "When you mention spring break, the first thing that comes to mind is that horrible murder that nice Scott Brundage was accused of down in Florida. Terrible, terrible thing that."

"Yes, it was awful." Issy glanced sideways at Ember. "What else do you remember about that time, Gladys?"

"Well, I'll tell you." The older lady leaned forward, her expression serious. "The elder Mr. Holland, Troy's father, was pretty darned upset about that whole episode. He didn't like his family name or business linked to that kind of scandal. I remember him telling Troy he'd never become president of the company if he was linked to such a salacious event." Gladys shook her head and sat back, her thin arms crossed. "Even refused to let the poor boy see Scott after that. They'd been close friends too. Of course, Troy was always so softhearted. He found ways to help Scott behind his father's back. Not that Troy and his father still didn't get into it something fierce sometimes. They tried to keep those fights behind closed doors, but in a place like this, the walls have ears."

"Was Jerry around during these fights?" Issy asked.

"Sure. But I'm telling you Jerry couldn't have had anything to do with that scandal. In fact, you asked if he took time off over spring break that year. And no, he didn't. He was here at the mill that whole time, helping with the internships. He didn't go on vacation until afterwards."

Ember nudged Issy again then walked with her over to a wall of photos behind Gladys's desk. "Are these pictures of the Holland family?"

Gladys stood and joined them, pointing to one particular photo. "Yes. See this photo right here? That's Jerry right there, with that summer's seven internship recipients—John, Max, Sally, Jane, Bob, Neal, and Carol."

"Wow!" Issy smiled down at the shorter woman. "I'm impressed you still remember all their names. I have trouble remembering what I ate for breakfast some days."

"Oh." Gladys gave Issy a coy wink. "I remember all sorts of things, ladies."

"I bet you do." Ember grinned.

The sound of a car screeching to a halt outside the front entrance had the trio swiveling toward the glass doors. Issy recognized Troy's black Cadillac idling at the curb and grabbed Ember's forearm. "We should be going."

"Oh, not yet," Gladys said, her tone disappointed. "We were having such a nice visit."

Len got out of the driver's side of the car, and from the grim expression on his face, he was anything but pleased.

"Don't pay any attention to Len," Gladys said, as if reading Issy's thoughts. "He's here for Troy anyway. Such a nice boy. Close as a brother to young Mr. Holland."

Len stopped at the security guard.

"That dumpster out there is overflowing and needs to be emptied today," Len said to the guard, his tone uncertain, as if he wasn't comfortable with giving orders. "Mr. Holland is not going to be happy. He was very clear about it being emptied on time this week."

"I made the call already, sir." The guard looked stricken. "I'm sorry it's such a mess, Mr. Childs. I do stay on top of the trash removal, but when I arrived this morning the garbage was strewn everywhere across the parking lot. My guess is those darn homeless folks were here foraging for stuff again." The guard shook his head. "Not to mention all those toads. They've taken up residence under the dumpster, which makes it harder for the trash collector to get the truck into proper position. Plus, they won't pick up the refuse unless everything's inside, so that's why they didn't do their usual pickup this morning. I had to gather all the garbage myself and get it back inside. They promised me they'll be back out this afternoon to take care of it, sir."

Len hung his head. Was he afraid of repercussions from Troy? Issy didn't remember much about him, but if he was anything like his father he might toe a hard line.

Len sighed. "Fine. These homeless people are becoming a nuisance. If you catch them out there again, call the police *before* Mr. Holland finds out they are getting in there. We don't want him to think we're not on top of things."

"Yes, sir," the guard said before scurrying back to his post at the front doors.

Turning to face them at last, Len looked genuinely surprised to see the three women staring back at him, as if he just now realized he wasn't alone. "Hello, Gladys. And two of the lovely Quinn cousins." He smiled. "What a pleasant surprise to see you this afternoon. To what do I owe this honor?"

"We were just in the area," Ember said, smiling a bit too brightly. "Thought we'd stop by and say hello to my old friend, Gladys."

"Yes, Gladys is a treasure, isn't she?" Len put his arm around the elderly receptionist. "She's become a part of our history here at Holland Mills. We couldn't do it without her."

Gladys blushed and swatted the younger man on the chest. "Flatterer."

Issy remembered the poor homeless people she'd met a few nights prior. They'd seemed nice and so proud of their dumpster finds. "Len, forgive me, but I heard what you said to that security guard. Please don't go too hard on the homeless for going through your trash. Most of them are good people who've fallen on bad times. They don't mean to hurt anyone, and isn't it better to have your old things put to good use than thrown away?"

"I'm all for helping the needy, Miss Quinn." Len scoffed. "But these people—"

"These people what?" Troy stepped off the elevators and headed across the lobby to where their group stood. "Issy and Ember, it's so good to see you." He shook their hands and seemed genuinely glad to have them there. "I'm so sorry to rush off, but Len and I are late for a meeting. Perhaps we can set up time to all go out for dinner, catch up on the old times, eh?"

"Sure," Issy mumbled as Troy and Len waved a hasty goodbye then fled back out the front doors and took off in the Cadillac. She blinked at the doors for several seconds before turning back to Gladys at last. "We need to be going too."

Gladys sighed and took a seat behind her desk once more, closing the box of chocolates and hiding the remainder in her desk drawer. "Fine. You young folks are all so busy these days. Well, you ladies have a great rest of your day and don't be strangers, you hear?"

"We hear." Ember waved to her old friend, as did Issy, then they headed back outside to the parking lot where Brown Betty sat at the end of a row of deserted spaces.

"I'm not sure if I should feel relieved or disappointed Jerry's not the killer," Issy said, once she and Ember were settled inside the truck.

"Look at it this way." Ember buckled her seat belt. "We now have one suspect crossed off the list."

"True." Issy slid on her sunglasses then pulled out of the parking lot. "But that means our killer is still on the loose."

"Hopefully there won't be a next victim." Ember shuddered.

"I don't know about that." Issy cranked up the heat. "What I do know is we need to follow up on our last lead—finding Marcy and figuring out what she was doing in Adele's house the other night."

Chapter Twenty-One

"Huh. Says here that Sarah Landers's body wasn't found right away," DeeDee said as she pulled more papers off the fax machine near her desk in the sheriff's office. "These eyewitness accounts seem a bit fuzzy too."

Dex snorted and settled back in his chair. After leaving The Main Squeeze, he'd bitten the bullet and headed back to the municipal building. He'd requested to be part of all these cases, and now he needed to do the job, even if the day was nice and he'd rather be at home with Gordon. Or better still, with Issy. He shook his head and focused on the case at hand. "Well, it was spring break. Most of those kids were probably drunk."

"True enough." Owen's rolling chair squeaked beneath his weight as he propped his feet up, leaned back, and grinned. "Anything else in all those faxes from Florida?"

"Nope." DeeDee straightened the stack of documents in her hand. "No new clues at all in what they've sent us so far."

Owen shifted in his seat. "Man. We need to catch a break here pretty soon. Right now, we've got two murders to solve. People around here are getting antsy for answers."

Dex glanced over the papers to the case information they had pinned to the cork board. So far all they had to go on were pictures of the murder scene. They had few leads and not many suspects. A familiar twinge of guilt pinched his gut.

Maybe Linda Brewer was right about her sister's murder. There hadn't been enough evidence against Scott for a guilty verdict. And the facts that Linda was murdered while looking into that old case and Adele—the accused's mother—found beaten in her home were no coincidence. It all had to be related.

If he could solve all three cases, maybe he could redeem himself for bungling that kidnapping case all those years ago. It was a long shot, but the only shot he had available at this point. He thumbed through the pages of witness testimony DeeDee handed him, frowning. "Something still seems off about these statements, though, drunk or not. I wonder if somebody paid these people off."

"Paid them to commit perjury, you mean?" Owen nodded, his expression thoughtful. "Could be. Hard to prove, though, this far out. That was ten years ago, and gathering bank statements from way back then for all those witnesses would be near impossible at this point."

"I can call our IT guy and see, if you want, boss," DeeDee offered.

"Sure, why not?" Owen clasped his hands behind his head. "Can't hurt to see."

While DeeDee made her call, Dex's phone rang. He set his papers aside and picked up the receiver. "Agent Dexter Nolan."

"Hey, Dex. Ursula at the ME's office. I've got a time of death for Linda Brewer."

"Great." He pulled out a pen and grabbed his notebook. "Go ahead."

"Based on the amount of mottling and rigor mortis, somewhere between eight and ten a.m."

"All right." He scribbled down the information. "Thanks, Ursula."

After hanging up, Dex waited until DeeDee was off the phone, then shared the information with her and Owen.

DeeDee frowned. "Pretty sure there's some surveillance cameras at that gas station down the street from the motel. Want me to have them pull the tapes from that morning, boss?"

"Yep." Owen dropped his feet to the floor and straightened, narrowing his gaze on Dex. "You ready to go talk to this Marcy gal?"

"Ready when you are." Dex stood and slipped on his leather jacket. "Want me to drive?"

"I'll take my own car." Owen pulled out his keys. "That way if another call comes in, I'm ready to go."

They headed for the door when DeeDee called out from behind them. "Just talked to the gas station manager, boss. He's going to pull the tapes for me now. I'll head over there and take a look. He said they don't point at the motel specifically, but the road in front of them isn't very busy, so at least we can see which cars came and went from that location during that time of day."

"Sounds good." Owen held the door for Dex. "Call me once you've got something."

"Will do, boss."

Dex had only driven a few blocks from the office when his cell phone rang. With one hand on the wheel, he reached over and answered, recognizing Stan's number immediately. He was the last person Dex wanted to talk to right now, but not answering wasn't an option. Stan would just keep calling. Resigned, Dex took a deep breath then put the call on speaker phone so he could talk without taking his eyes off the road. "Agent Nolan."

"Dex? It's Stan. Listen, I've got some exciting news. There's some new movie mogul who I'm pretty sure is going to set up a paranormal smoke screen in Silver Hollow."

While Stan babbled on about his new hunch, Dex tuned him out and focused on the road ahead. He vaguely remembered seeing some hotshot guy at the next table when he'd been at The Main Squeeze earlier with Gray. The guy had reeked of West Coast swagger and Hollywood schmaltz and looked completely out of place in their quiet New England town.

He stopped at a red light and stared out the window while Stan rambled.

"This movie business is a perfect front for actual paranormals. Can you imagine?" Stan said, his voice more animated than Dex could ever remember.

And yeah. He could imagine paranormals. One paranormal to be exact. A woman with seafoam-green eyes and bouncy strawberry-blond curls and a smile that could light up the whole universe.

The light turned green, and the driver behind Dex honked. He waved in the rearview mirror and accelerated.

"The guy makes movies about werewolves and vampires, Dex. Think about it. No wonder he's moving to Silver Hollow, this little out-of-the-way town, so he can have actual real werewolves and vampires in his films!"

Dex shook his head and turned down the road that led toward the bridge where the homeless lived. He could see Owen's squad car in the distance, already waiting. Tension cramped his gut as he pulled up to the berm behind Owen's car. Stan could very well be right about this movie guy coming to town for the paranormals, especially given what Dex now knew about the place. But he'd sworn his allegiance to protecting these people, and he'd rather die than see any of them taken into Area 59 for questioning, which was exactly what Stan wanted.

With a sigh, he picked up his phone and took the call off speaker. "Hey, Stan. This all sounds super fascinating, but I need to go. I'm with Owen, and we're going to question a suspect in the town's latest murder case. I'll definitely look into this movie guy, though, once my schedule lightens. Right now, I'm knee-deep in this murder case. I'll talk to you later, okay?"

Owen got out of his squad car and waved. Dex waved back, using the first excuse that popped into his mind to end the call with Stan. "I don't want the local cops to get suspicious I'm not following through on this case like a regular FBI agent would. Talk to you soon."

Chapter Twenty-Two

"Hey, isn't that Dex's Buick?" Ember pointed out the windshield of Brown Betty as Issy pulled over to the berm of the road near the bridge. They'd decided to put in a concerted Quinn family effort into finally finding and questioning Marcy. "And that looks like Owen's squad car too."

"They must be here working on the case." Issy cut the engine and got out of the truck just as Raine pulled her Jeep in behind her. She got out too—along with Gray, who rode with her from the greenhouse—and began to unload the plants she'd brought for the homeless people. Issy and Ember walked over to help carry them all. "Did you have a chance to enchant these?"

"Sure did." Raine grinned over the top of the plant in her arms. "Guaranteed to make folks more talkative."

"These are nice." Gray hoisted two huge pots beneath each of his beefy arms. "Those poor folks down there could use something to cheer them up."

"Agreed." Ember grabbed another, smaller plant from the back of the Jeep. "Plus, Issy will get to see her favorite man crush too."

"He's not my man crush." Issy had to tamp down the rush of excitement that sizzled through her at the prospect of seeing Dex again. "We're just friends."

"Sure you are." Raine winked.

"What are you Quinns doing here?" Owen said, climbing up the embankment from the riverbed below. "This is official police business. Civilians shouldn't be here. It could be dangerous."

"Hey, Issy," Dex said, rushing up beside Owen. His eager grin and the spark of heat in his hazel eyes chased away Owen's chilly greeting. He cocked his chin toward the plants in her arms. "Are you guys bringing those for the homeless?"

"What?" Issy blinked at him for a moment, unable to concentrate on anything besides his handsome face. Her vow to keep him at arm's length because it looked like he was leaving town dissolved. Ember nudged her in the ribs and gave her a keep-up look, jarring Issy from her daydreams of her and Dex in a bungalow all their own. "Oh, yeah. We thought they'd make a nice gift. Something to brighten their day."

"Come on, Owen, you know these people aren't dangerous." Raine frowned at Owen over the top of the plant in her arms. "Just down on their luck. And you should be glad we're here. They like us. We've built a rapport with them. How many of your questions did they answer, huh?"

Owen gave an exasperated sigh and looked away. "None."

"That's good, then," Issy said, her gaze still stuck on Dex. "They're more apt to talk if we're here."

"She's got a point," Dex said, moving to stand beside Issy. "The Quinns got far more information out of them the other night than we did today. Maybe if we go back down there with them along, they'll see that we're only there to help and they'll open up to us."

Owen shook his head and exhaled loudly. "Fine. But I still don't think we should be letting civilians into our investigation."

"Cool." Raine handed one of her plants to Owen, and Dex took one of Issy's, and they all headed back down the embankment to the river's edge, following the shoreline until they reached the homeless encampment under the bridge. In the daylight, it was easier to make out the various cardboard box shelters and backpacks strewn about. Ed spotted them from his position near a large campfire at the center of the shanty village and came out to greet them.

"Back again, eh?" He eyed Raine's plants with suspicion. "You planning on adding to the forest?"

"No." Issy passed her plant over to Ed. "We thought these might brighten your day."

"I own the greenhouse and landscaping business in town. I'm happy to send my plants to those in need." Raine passed out the plants to the homeless gathered around them now. "These are hardy perennial lilies. They'll bloom each year as long as you take good care of them."

Ed grinned through his scraggly beard. "Thanks. We don't get many gifts down here these days." He leaned to the side slightly and spotted Owen and Dex behind Gray, and his smile fell. "What are those cops doing back here again?"

"They're friends," Issy said. "Take a whiff of those lilies, Ed. They smell divine." She shot Raine a look. "Seriously. My cousin has a special touch when it comes to plants."

The homeless guy gave her a skeptical stare then slowly bent and sniffed one of the white flowers on his plant. Soon, he took another sniff, then another. The Quinn cousins' gazes met, and they all visibly relaxed as Ed's tense posture slumped and his grin returned.

"Yeah," Ed said. "These smell fantastic."

Issy glanced over at Owen and gave him a slight nod.

Owen stepped forward and handed his plant off to Issy. "Sir, we'd like to ask you some questions about Scott Brundage, if you don't mind."

"Nope." Ed took another smell of his flowers, his grin widening. "Don't mind at all."

Dex raised an inquiring brow at Issy but thankfully didn't say a word.

"First, sir, can you tell us where we can find a gal named Marcy?" Owen took out his notepad and a pen.

"Is she in trouble?" Ed asked, though his tone remained placid.

"No, sir. We just want to talk to her."

Ed turned and glanced toward a nearby cardboard box. Issy nudged Dex and pointed, and the two of them inched closer to the box. Shuffling sounds and breathing could be heard from inside, and Dex held a finger to his lips for Issy to keep quiet. She nodded and held her breath as Dex rounded the front corner of the large, refrigerator-sized box. Just as he reached the front flap, however, the person inside darted out and took off for the forest.

Issy spotted the same slight frame, same striped hoodie from that night at Adele's.

Marcy.

This time, though, Dex managed to catch up with her before she got lost in the woods. He grabbed her arm and turned her around just as Issy reached them.

Marcy was crying and struggling, something square clutched to her chest. "Let me go!"

"We need to ask you some questions," Issy said, doing her best to keep her voice low and calm to ease the agitated girl. Narrowing her gaze, she realized the object Marcy was holding was a photo album. "Please, Marcy. We only want to help Scott."

"Scott's dead," Marcy sobbed. "He's beyond help now."

"Where did you get the album?" Dex asked, still gripping Marcy's arm firmly.

"Just arrest me, okay? That's why you're here, isn't it?" She sniffled. "They were going to throw it out anyway."

"May I see it?" Issy asked gently and held out her hand.

After a few tense moments, Marcy reluctantly handed it over. Issy frowned down at the cover. "Why would you want someone else's photo album?"

"It's not someone else's," Marcy said. "Those pictures are of Scott."

Issy opened the album and flipped through page after page of Scott Brundage in better days. Happy, sunny, family-and-friend-filled days. She glanced up and met Dex's gaze. "This must be part of what was missing from Adele's bookshelves." She looked back to Marcy. "Where did you find it?"

Marcy's uncertain gaze flicked between the two of them.

"Tell us, Marcy," Dex said, his tone reassuring. "You won't get in trouble, I promise."

The homeless girl slumped a bit. "At the paper mill. I didn't think anyone would mind me taking it, since it was in their dumpster."

Several feet away, Owen's phone chirped with an incoming call. He excused himself and stepped aside to take it. "Yeah. DeeDee, what did you find?"

Issy turned her attention away from Owen and back to Marcy, holding up the photo album. "Is this why you were at Adele's the other night?"

"Yes." Marcy swiped the sleeve of her dirty hoodie under her nose. "When I went to the funeral I saw she had all these nice pictures of Scott." Marcy gestured around their makeshift village scattered with old milk crates and tarps. "As you can see, we don't get many nice things down here. And I have nothing left from the man I love."

Pity swelled tight in Issy's chest. She couldn't imagine the hardships this poor young girl had gone through, then to lose her lover so tragically, with nothing but memories to keep close. It broke Issy's heart. If anything like that ever happened to Dex, she wasn't sure what she'd do, how she'd cope...

"What?" Owen said, from the sidelines, his voice louder now. "Well, were you at least able to check the tapes from that morning—"

"Anyway," Marcy continued, drawing Issy's attention back to her. "When I asked his mom at the funeral if I could have a couple of the pictures, she wouldn't give me any." Marcy's face scrunched again, and her tears flowed anew. "Adele never did like me. We argued about the pictures at the funeral, even."

Issy caught Dex's glance again, the puzzle pieces coming together in her mind. That must've been the fight Troy mentioned at the wake.

"So you broke in later to get them?" Dex asked, frowning.

"Yes," Marcy admitted. "I mean, no. I tried to get in, but I couldn't."

"Don't lie, Marcy," Dex said, his voice harsher now. "We both saw you at Adele Brundage's house that night. You ran from me. Did you go there earlier in the week and beat Adele when she wouldn't give you the pictures?"

"What? No! The first time I went there ever was the night I ran into you, but the pictures weren't there."

Dex folded his arms across his chest. "I think you're lying. You just said you tried to get in but couldn't, and you were clearly in the house that night."

"Huh?" Marcy gave him a confused scowl. "No. That wasn't Adele's I couldn't get into. I thought you meant the funeral parlor. And I wasn't breaking in. I thought maybe the door was still open, but when I tried the handle it set off the alarm." She shook her head. "I didn't break the door at his mom's house either. All I did was slip a bobby pin into the lock. Easy-peasy. I didn't mean any harm, I swear. I figured the photos might still be inside. All I wanted were some pictures of Scott to remember him by, and since she was already dead I figured no one would miss them. But when I got inside, the pictures weren't there."

Dex shifted on his feet looking like he didn't believe her. "Right, because they were in a dumpster instead, where you conveniently found them. And just what were you doing in the dumpster?"

Marcy looked down at her feet. "Lots of us rummage through dumpsters. You can get things to sell or trade. I go to the one at the paper mill for scrap paper and old office supplies. I couldn't believe the albums were in there. Weird, huh?"

Owen ended his call and stalked over to them, his expression angry.

Dex stepped back, still holding on to Marcy, and raised a brow at Issy.

"Well, I just talked to DeeDee. She watched those tapes from the gas station down the street from Linda Brewer's motel. Apparently only five cars drove down that road within the timeframe the ME gave us. A white Ford Taurus, a yellow Volkswagen Beetle, a maroon Toyota Camry, a black Cadillac, and a black Prius."

"Did she get license plate numbers?" Dex asked.

While the men talked, Issy opened the photo album again and flipped through more pages, her mind racing with information. Five cars, two murders, one homeless thief trying to save photos of her dead love. She blinked down at the new page of pictures, her gaze narrowing on one photo in the corner. Was that a palm tree?

Pulse tripping, Issy looked up at Dex with wide eyes. "I think I found something."

"Yeah?" He stepped in closer beside her while Owen did the same on the other side. "What?"

"Look at these pictures." She pointed to the one with the palm tree and a few others with beachy-looking scenes. "I think these might have come from that spring break trip they all took ten years ago."

Dex leaned in closer and squinted. "I think you're right. That sure looks like Florida to me."

"Turn the page," Owen said then waited while Issy did. "Yep." He pointed to another photo, this one of the front of a resort. "See that sign? It's the Tropic Ranch Hotel. The same place Sarah Landers was staying ten years ago when she was murdered."

Breath lodged in her throat, Issy continued to flip through the pages of the album, a new idea forming in her head. "Did you say there was a black Cadillac on the surveillance footage from the gas station?"

"Yep," Owen said. "Why?"

"I think I know who our murderer is. Look at this." Issy tapped on another picture in the album. "If I'm not mistaken, the guy behind this person in the Hawaiian shirt is Troy Holland."

"Sorry, I'm not following." Owen stepped back with a frown. "It's common knowledge Troy and Scott were good friends, especially back then. They hung out all the time."

"True, but during this particular spring break, Troy and Len were supposedly helping out with internships at his father's paper mill. Or so they said. In fact, I think they made it a point to let people know they weren't in Florida that week back then. Gladys at the plant even corroborated it. Why would they not want to admit to being in Florida?"

"Dang it! They must've all been covering for Troy," Owen said. "Troy must've seen these pictures at Scott's funeral and freaked out."

"So maybe it was *him* that broke into Adele's house too," Dex added. "He needed to take those albums to erase all the evidence of his involvement in Sarah Landers's murder. But Adele probably confronted him, and he killed her to keep her quiet. Explains how the album turned up in a dumpster at the paper mill later too."

Issy waved her cousins over and filled them in on what they'd discovered.

Gray made a face. "Why would Troy toss that in his own company's trash, though? Not very bright for a smart guy. You'd think he'd burn such damning evidence instead."

"Maybe with all the investigations going on he didn't want to get caught burning anything. Or maybe he had to dump it quick," Ember said. "When Issy and I were there earlier, Len came in and was complaining about some screwup by the sanitation department and their dumpster not being emptied on time. Seemed like he was afraid Troy would be mad."

"Oh, right!" Issy nodded. "The guard had said the homeless had been rooting around inside the dumpster when he got there and trash was spilled everywhere in the parking lot. Must have been Marcy he saw going through the trash. Troy could've easily disposed of the album in there, thinking the garbage truck would haul it away and mash it to a pulp. Once that happened, no one would ever find the evidence."

They all stood silent for several moments, but something was still bugging Issy. She couldn't quite place it, until... "That's it!" She snapped her fingers. "I knew something was strange about those photos Gladys showed us, Ember. She specifically said Troy and Len had stayed to help with the internships that summer, but when she showed us those pictures on the wall of the candidates chosen, Jerry was in them, but not Troy!"

"Oh my gosh!" Ember covered her mouth. "You're right."

"That also explains why Linda Brewer was holding that photo in her hand, the one of the visitor's badge," Dex said, glancing at Owen. "It wasn't a clue that pointed to Jerry as her killer. It was a clue pointing toward the paper mill—and Troy is the mill's president."

"Man." Raine shook her head, her expression disgusted. "I can't believe Troy lied all those years ago to avoid going to prison for murder and let his friend take the blame instead."

"That explains why he's always been so nice. Buying meals and trying to help him out. Guilty conscience," Ember said.

"Well, I'll tell you one thing," Owen said, pulling out his phone again and turning toward his car. "He might've gotten away with it all those years ago, but he won't get away with it now!"

Dex grabbed the photo album from Issy and rushed off after Owen, the two of them sidestepping and jumping over toads on the way to their cars.

Chapter Twenty-Three

"What's going on?" Ed asked, walking over to them, the plant gone and the tension back in his posture. "Marcy, are you all right?"

From atop the embankment, the wail of sirens and the screech of tires sounded as Dex and Owen took off to find Troy. Issy forced a smile and did her best to keep her voice calm. "The police think they may have found out who killed Adele Brundage and Linda Brewer."

"Who?" Ed put his arm around Marcy's shoulders and pulled her into his side.

"Troy Holland." Gray crossed his arms and scowled.

Ed cursed under his breath as Marcy buried her face in his broad chest. "He and Len used to come down here sometimes to visit Scott." Ed's bushy brows drew together as his expression darkened. "In fact, I saw that fancy Cadillac here the day Scott died."

Marcy sniffed and raised her head to look at Issy. "Scott was trying to get clean. He hadn't touched any drugs in a couple of days, but the police thought he'd fallen off the wagon and overdosed. He didn't, though. I swear he didn't."

The Quinn cousins exchanged a look, and Issy leaned closer to Marcy. "Do you think Scott was starting to remember things from that spring break trip? Was that why Troy would want to kill him?"

"I don't think so." She wiped her nose on the sleeve of her hoodie again. "At least he never said anything to me if he did. But Troy used to give Scott money. I was always suspicious of that. Though maybe they wanted to keep him hooked on the drugs to stop him from saying or remembering something he shouldn't." She blinked back more tears. "Way I figure, whoever killed him probably heard he was going clean and made sure he would never remember anything again."

Marcy's sobs started again, and Issy did her best to soothe the poor girl, while Raine frowned at them both then backed away. "We should go."

Gray checked his watch then followed behind her. "I should go too. Booked solid with hair appointments the rest of the night. You ladies okay to get home?"

"Yep." Issy glanced up at him. With Owen and Dex on their way to arrest Troy, things felt safer. "We'll be fine. Go ahead and go back to work."

With a wave, Gray started back up the embankment after Raine.

Ember stayed by Issy's side and tried to help comfort Marcy. "Don't worry, sweetie. Justice will finally be done."

"Yes," Issy repeated, staring at all the toads still hopping everywhere. Given they'd solved the murders, she'd kind of expected the creatures to disappear immediately. Then again, with the vehemence attached to Adele's initial curse, maybe it would take a little longer. Perhaps after Owen and Dex arrested Troy...

"They took the photo album," Marcy sobbed, still inconsolable. "Why did they have to take it? Now I have nothing to remind me of Scott. Do you think they'll give it back to me?"

"I don't know." Issy patted Marcy's hand. Deep inside, she seriously doubted they'd return the album anytime soon, if at all, but she didn't want to risk upsetting the poor homeless girl more. "Maybe."

"I wonder if that nice guy I talked to at the funeral would give me some of his pictures," Marcy said, her tears stopping momentarily and her expression lighting. "He said he had a bunch at home. Even said he might have some pictures of Scott on an old camera he had back at that time."

Issy frowned. "What guy was that?"

"That older guy who breaks stuff without touching it."

Issy met Ember's startled gaze, and they both said in unison, "Jerry Blaisdale?"

"Um, yeah." Marcy scrunched her nose. "I think he did say his first name was Jerry."

"It can't be him, though," Ember said over the top of Marcy's head. "He's out of town."

"Really?" Marcy took the tissue Issy offered her and blew her nose. "That's weird. Because when I went by his house after I found that album in the dumpster, a car was parked in his driveway."

"Are you sure it was him?" Issy asked, her gaze narrowed.

"Not sure. I didn't go in because of all the loud crashes inside the house."

Sitting back on her haunches, Issy tried to make sense of these new clues. Could Jerry be back from his vacation already? It was possible. Maybe it had only been a short, two-day deal. If he *had* come back early, though, he could blow Troy's alibi out of the water, which Troy Holland would know.

But Jerry could have done that ten years ago during the trial. Why would Troy be worried about that now? Maybe he was afraid that with Jerry's new venture as a PI he'd want to crack a big case to prove how good he was. And what better case to crack than a ten-year-old unsolved murder?

Suddenly, those loud crashes at Jerry's house took on a more ominous tone. Jerry Blaisdale could be in trouble—or worse.

The police were heading to arrest Troy, but they'd never think to look for him at Jerry's. She pulled out her cell phone and called DeeDee, then tried to reach Owen, but there was no answer.

"We need to go," Issy said, without a second thought.

Ember gave Marcy a last squeeze then followed her cousin up the embankment to their vehicle. "Where are we off to in such a hurry?"

"Jerry's house. There's a real possibility he's in grave danger and he'll need our powerful magic to help him."

Chapter Twenty-Four

"Would someone please tell me what the heck is going on?" Troy Holland demanded. "If you don't explain what I'm being held for right now, I'll have my attorneys sue this entire department for false imprisonment. I'll have your badges. Your careers will be over."

Dex stared at the irate guy across the interrogation table, his expression as impassive as his tone. Those threats were the same ones any other criminal made when their back was against the wall. The only difference this time was that Troy Holland and his family might have the clout to follow through. Still, Dex wouldn't let that stop him from doing what was right. He'd allowed his duty to override his common sense once before, with disastrous results.

"Answer the question, Mr. Holland," Dex said, his voice flat and his words even. "Why are you missing from the photos of the internships candidates that summer ten years ago? According to your company records and witness testimony taken at the time of Sarah Landers's murder, you were supposed to be on-site, here in Silver Hollow, helping with orientation for the new interns."

Troy sighed and hung his head, the fight seeming to go out of him briefly. "Okay, look. Maybe I did sneak out and go down to the Tropic Ranch with my friends that spring. We were young and stupid and impetuous. My dad was so busy back then, he didn't notice I was even around much, except when I did something wrong or didn't perform up to his impossibly high standards. Then, of course, he was all over me like white on rice. I wanted one last bit of fun before reality took it all away. So, I didn't see any harm in shirking my responsibilities for a week. I went down there and had a blast with my friends. Foolish? Yes. A crime? Hardly."

"A crime was committed that week, though, Mr. Holland," Owen said from the shadows of the room. "A serious crime."

Troy cursed under his breath and slumped back in his seat, his eyes squeezed shut. "I know where you're going with this, but I'm telling you, I didn't kill that girl! I would never kill anyone!"

"Is that so?" Owen pushed away from the wall and walked over, setting an iPad down in front of Troy on the table then pushing Play. Footage from the gas station surveillance cameras streamed on endless loop, a vehicle zooming past the camera at high speed. "And

I suppose you're going to tell me next this isn't your car?" Owen straightened and crossed his arms, his expression incredulous. "Pretty sure you're the only guy in town with a top-of-the-line, fully loaded, fancy black Cadillac like that."

"Yeah, that looks like my car." Troy glanced from the iPad to Owen then back again, his expression confused. "So what?"

Dex narrowed his gaze on their suspect, searching for any signs of deception in his body language, any sign at all that the guy was lying. There were none he could see, but that didn't mean anything in and of itself. If the guy had killed once already and gotten away with it, then he was good at misleading people. Very good. "That car was seen going to the Route Nine Motel this morning around the time Linda Brewer was killed."

Troy scowled. "Who is Linda Brewer? What time was this?"

"This morning between eight and ten," Owen said.

"Well, those cameras must be wrong, then, because I was nowhere near that area this morning." Troy shook his head and sat up a little straighter. "I was downtown, in a meeting with the mayor until at least twelve thirty. You can find it on the calendar on my phone." He met Dex's gaze, a brow raised. "You know, the one you confiscated. Check it. And if you still don't believe me, then call the mayor's office."

Owen gestured for Dex to join him out in the hallway. Once the door was closed, the sheriff scrubbed a hand over his face and frowned. "Do you think he's telling the truth?"

Dex glanced back into the room uneasily. "Be stupid to bluff about that. It's pretty easy to verify."

"Well, if it wasn't Troy, who was it then?"

"Let me think a minute." Dex rested his shoulder against the wall and went over all the details of the case in his head. If they'd ruled out Jerry and now Troy, the only other person with motive and access to Troy's car was... "Len Childs."

"Len?" Owen said, realization dawning on his face. "Yes. That makes sense. He and Troy were each other's alibi during the Sarah Landers murder investigation."

"Yep. And if Troy snuck out and headed to Florida ten years ago, it's a sure bet Len was there too. He's like Troy's shadow."

"Wait a minute. From what the Quinn gals said, Len was the one who saw the homeless people in the dumpster earlier, so—"

"Crap!" Dex rushed down the hallway toward his desk to grab his gun and car keys. "If Len put two and two together and realizes one of the homeless took that photo album, then he might try to go after them. Issy and her cousins are still down there at that shantytown. We need to warn them."

Owen hurried after him, grabbing his own weapon and shoving it in the holster at his waist before following Dex to the door. "I'll go to Len's place in case he's there."

"Wait!" DeeDee yelled from behind them, but they were already out the door.

Dex rushed to his Buick and started the engine, barely checking in the rearview mirror to see Owen turn off in the direction of Len Childs's. He pressed on, lights and sirens going. Traffic stopped or slowed to allow him to pass, but the toads were another thing entirely. Every few feet, Dex would have to slam on the brakes or swerve to avoid ending up with toad guts everywhere on his vehicle.

It took him twice as long as usual to get back to the bridge due to all the unexpected stops. His heart was in his throat by the time he finally pulled over onto the gravel berm and got out. Both Issy's pickup and her cousin's Jeep were gone, but knowing her, she might still be down there with the homeless. And if anything happened to Issy, he couldn't live with himself, couldn't live with the knowledge he'd failed twice to save those entrusted to his care.

Flashbacks filtered into his mind of that kid. So young, so innocent, so undeserving of what had happened to him. All of it was Dex's fault. He hadn't listened to his gut at the time. He'd followed orders from his superiors and sat tight, instead of going to search for that poor kid like he'd wanted to. That kid had died because of Dex's inaction.

If Issy died, Dex would never recover.

There was no way he could live with the soul-crushing guilt, the failure.

With heels crunching and skidding on the loose stones, he rushed down the embankment and over to the burly bearded guy they'd questioned earlier. Ed, that was the guy's name. He stalked to the fire barrel the man was standing at with his back to Dex and grabbed him by the arm.

Ed swiveled fast, his fists up, ready to fight. Considering the guy had a good fifty pounds on Dex, the outcome wouldn't have been in his favor. He was too far gone to care about his own personal safety at that point, though. All that mattered now, all that he cared about, was finding and protecting the woman he...

What?

Liked... Loved...

No. Dex wasn't ready to go there yet, despite the burst of warmth that word caused to flare inside him. He and Issy barely knew each other. And yes, the attraction was definitely there, but something more? That remained to be seen. He just prayed he wasn't too late to find out.

"Where's Issy?" Dex asked, his words rushing out on a tide of adrenaline and fear. He craned his neck to see if he could spot Issy's bright strawberry-blond curls, but there was nothing. His heart plummeted to his toes, and his pulse hammered loudly in his ears. If he was too late to save her...

"What?" Ed asked, obviously suspicious. "Who's Issy?"

Dex gave the homeless man a harsh stare, his fists clenched to keep from punching the guy. "Issy Quinn. She and her cousins were here with us earlier."

"Oh." Ed grinned, his teeth barely visible through his thick, matted beard. "Right. Yeah, the Quinns left a little while ago. Those two gals were sure in a hurry too. Said they needed to go check on someone named Jerry."

Dex turned and ran for his car.

Chapter Twenty-Five

Issy swerved to the curb near Jerry Blaisdale's house and cut the engine. She'd expected to see Troy Holland's black Cadillac in the driveway but instead spotted only Jerry's red Honda Civic. Why would he be home from Bermuda so soon?

She and Ember got out and locked the truck then carefully made their way across the street to the house. There were no lights on, and all the drapes were pulled. Looked like no one was home.

Ember peeked through one of the windows on the side of the home and waved Issy over. "The inside's a mess."

"Jerry does have a problem with his spells," Issy said, squinting through the gauzy curtains at the chaos inside. Papers, shattered glass, and broken furniture were strewn everywhere. "Maybe the stress of this investigation made it worse. That would explain the loud noises Marcy said she heard too."

"Hmm." Ember stepped back and fussed with her turtleneck cashmere sweater. "Or maybe we're too late and Troy Holland was already here to take care of Jerry."

Sighing, Issy headed around toward the breezeway near the back of the house. "Either way, I don't think we have a choice. We need to go inside. Jerry could be in there and might need help."

"Agreed." Ember crept quietly behind Issy. "Do you want me to do the unlocking spell?"

"I got it." Issy stood back from the door and rubbed her hands together. Eyes closed, she began reciting the spell in her head, building her power until her skin tingled and her heart thudded and then...

Air rushed past Issy's cheeks, followed by a loud, surprised gasp.

That wasn't part of the spell.

"What's going on, Em?" she asked her cousin.

No answer.

"Ember?"

Nothing.

Issy peeked one eye open and noticed two things simultaneously. First, the door to the breezeway was open. Second, Ember was nowhere to be found.

Springing into action, Issy rushed through the open doorway and peered through the murky darkness inside. Perhaps that strong breeze had pushed the door open and Ember had headed into the house. No, that couldn't have been right. Ember wouldn't have rushed in without Issy. Pulse quickening, Issy tiptoed down the dark breezeway, keeping one hand on the stucco wall to orient herself. "Ember?" she whispered. "Are you in here?"

She turned a corner and heard another gasp, this time accompanied by a grunt and a squeak. There was moonlight streaming in through the front windows, and she could make out the silhouette of a man holding another person against their will. Issy blinked several times to clear her vision. By the time her eyes adjusted, her heart had nosedived to somewhere near her toes. It was Len Childs—not Troy—leaning against a mirrored wall in Jerry's living room. He had his arm wrapped around Ember's neck, holding her captive, and a gun pointed at her temple.

"Let her go!" Issy shouted, though she knew it was useless. As useless as her magic would be in here. She didn't know if Len knew anything about magic, but if he had, he'd been smart. By leaning against that mirrored wall, there was no way Issy could risk casting a spell against him without the possibility of it boomeranging back at her—especially with that gun so close to Ember's head. The results could be deadly.

Her original plans in tatters, Issy's confidence waned. She and Ember had charged over here with the belief their magic would defend them against whatever Troy Holland might throw at them. She hadn't thought it through and considered all the possible outcomes. Like a big fat magic-inhibiting mirror on one wall.

"You nosy Quinns just can't mind your own business, can you?" Len snarled, his face twisted with rage. "Now I'll have to kill both of you too."

Issy met his gaze, doing her best not to let her terror show. "It was you? You killed Sarah Landers ten years ago?"

"She had it coming." Len squeezed his arm tighter around Ember's throat, and she clawed at his forearm, struggling for breath. "Just like the two of you."

Panicked, Issy glanced into the open kitchen nearby. It too was in shambles—drawers on the floor, utensils tossed willy-nilly all over the place. She looked back at Len, working off her suspicions. "You've been looking for something."

"What have you done with Jerry Blaisdale?" Ember managed to say, still struggling against Len's hold.

Len snorted. "I figured you gals would have doped it out by now. I was the one who sent Jerry on vacation. Made up that whole story about it being a benefit from the paper mill and all. And good old Jerry... well, he's so stupid, he bought it the same as he did ten years ago."

"Why?" Issy asked, sure she already had a good idea of the answer but wanting to keep him talking just the same. If he was distracted, that meant he was less likely to hurt Ember.

"Why? To get Jerry out of here so I could look for the camera I gave him after that Florida trip during spring break." Len shook his head. "I told Troy to ditch that camera, but no. He said his dad gave it to him and it had sentimental value, so he gave it to Jerry instead. I told him it could blow our cover, show we were down there goofing around instead of being up here at work like we were supposed to be, but Troy wouldn't budge, and since Jerry was a camera buff and it was a new fancy model, he figured we could stash it with him until everything blew over. Jerry thought he was being nice, and he never figured out the *real* reason."

"And Troy never asked for it back after all these years?"

"Oh, he did. I was nice enough to get it back for him. Well, at least that's what Troy thought. See, I didn't want to call attention to the camera. Didn't want to raise Jerry's suspicions, so I simply went out and got the exact same model and pretended it was the one he'd given to Jerry. The exact one his father had given him."

"So the real evidence of what happened to Sarah Landers has been hidden under Jerry Blaisdale's roof the whole time? And no one but you knew it was there."

"Yep." Len flashed a self-satisfied grin. "Brilliant, eh? Good thing for me there wasn't any Facebook or social media back then. Otherwise all those dumb college kids would've been posting second-by-second updates of what they were doing every single minute of the day."

Issy shook her head. "That's why you destroyed all the other cameras."

"Of course." Len winked, and a cold shiver of fear ran through Issy. This guy wasn't remorseful at all over what he'd done. In fact, he was proud of killing that girl. "I figured if I ruined the cameras, the pictures inside them would be ruined too. So I paid some ditzy blond to toss all the cameras into the pool one night at a party. I tried to get Troy to do it to save us some money, but he was too much of a goodie-goodie to go along with the plan."

"You were taking quite a risk that Jerry wouldn't look at the pictures and figure things out," Issy said.

"I erased them, so I knew Jerry would never find them. But I know the cops have ways to recover erased data. I didn't want the police getting that camera. Ten years ago, Jerry took it on the trumped-up vacation with him but turns out that wasn't even necessary. The cops never even questioned Jerry or knew about Troy's camera. But now that things were heating up again, I figured I better find that camera and destroy it."

"So Troy helped you cover up the murder?" Issy needed to keep him talking, get him away from that mirror, if possible. That way she could blast him with her magic and get this horrible situation back under control. "Doesn't sound like a very good guy to me."

"Troy never knew about me killing that girl." Len scoffed. "He thought I was just keen to cover up our secret trip during spring break so his dad wouldn't get mad. It served my purposes, so I let him keep thinking that. Hyped it up too, saying I'd overheard his dad say that if he ever found out about a scandal, he'd disown Troy, cut him out of the paper mill and his inheritance. Well, that was more than enough to keep good-boy Troy on my tight leash.

"The fact his dad had flown all the way down to Florida to bring us home and hustled us away in secret only reinforced the idea in his head." Len shrugged. "After that, it was easy enough to play on Troy's fears and insecurities to get him to help me cover our tracks at the paper mill and establish our alibi as interns once the story of Sarah Landers's murder broke. I thought everything was scrubbed clean too, until I found Troy's camera shoved in my backpack. That took a little ingenuity, but I convinced Troy to let Jerry keep the camera for him. We made up some story about it, and good old Jerry was too stupid to connect the dots and understand the significance."

"But why did you send Jerry on vacation again?" Issy inched to the side, hoping Len might follow suit and move away from the mirrored wall. Then she might have a chance of rescuing Ember. "Why not just ask him for the camera back?"

"Jerry was meeting with that private detective. He was all worked up about investigating the case. He was dumb, but I knew he would get suspicious if I suddenly asked about that camera now. I figured if I killed the guy, the cops would lock up this house as a crime scene like they did Adele's. Couldn't get what I needed if it was locked up, so I sent him to Bermuda instead. Still can't quite believe the poor schmuck fell for the same con twice."

So that's why Gladys had seemed confused about the trips. It wasn't because they weren't offered to her, they weren't offered to anyone.

"So you killed Adele too?"

"Had to. I saw the photos at Scott's funeral. I had forgotten about that stupid old instant camera someone had at spring break until I saw pictures of Scott on that spring break vacation at his funeral. Then

I heard that scraggly girlfriend of Scott's asking Adele for some box of photos. I couldn't take the chance that one of them would show my face."

"So you broke in and bludgeoned an old woman?"

"I wouldn't have had to if she'd just stayed in her bedroom. I was quiet as a mouse. Wanted time to go through all the books so I could just take the photos. I heard her moving around in the hall. I hid, and when she went into the kitchen, I came up behind her. She was a mean old thing, and something weird happened in there. There was a ghost or… something floating around. Spooked me so I grabbed anything that looked like it could have photos and ran. Got a bunch of crap like appointment books, but also got the photos."

"Why'd you dump them in the dumpster?"

Len scowled. "Stupid homeless people screwed me again on that. I put the albums in right before the truck was supposed to come. Would have gone to the landfill and been buried under a ton of garbage long before anyone even thought to look for them if that meddlesome girlfriend didn't do her dumpster-diving routine."

"I still don't understand why you killed Scott, though," Issy said.

Len made a face. "He's the one person I didn't kill. He really did kill himself. Maybe he overdosed by mistake, I have no idea. Honestly, if he hadn't, I would never have known about those photos and we could have all gone on with our lives, fat, dumb, and happy. But now I've had to kill two other people, and it looks like I'm gonna kill two more."

"Why did you kill Sarah Landers in the first place?" Ember squeaked out.

Len gave a derisive snort. "The girls always liked Troy and Scott better. Never liked me. When we hit the beaches at spring break, that Sarah was all over Scott like white on rice. I tried talking to her, but she wouldn't give me the time of day." Len squeezed Ember tighter, and she gagged, her feet scrabbling on the hardwood floor. Issy held her breath, desperate to figure out how to save her cousin. "But I got Sarah to pay attention to me in the end."

Through the dim light, Ember met Issy's eyes, and a silent understanding passed between them. Ember ceased her struggles and gazed up at Len, batting her eyelashes. "That's not true, Len. We always liked you."

He scrunched his nose and looked down at her. "You did?"

"Yes," Issy chimed in, moving a tad closer to them. She forced a smile. "And look at all this stuff you've kept covered up for years. You're so clever, Len. Isn't that right, Ember?"

"Oh yeah." Ember straightened slightly as Len's hold on her throat loosened. "No one ever suspected you killed Sarah Landers. We all thought it was that drug addict, Scott. And don't worry, we won't tell anyone either, Len. Will we, Issy?"

"No. My lips are sealed." Issy moved closer still, thinking if she could flatter him enough to let Ember go completely then she could hit him with a somnambulism spell. A sleeping incantation would knock them all out for a while, but at least it wouldn't hurt anyone if it bounced back through the mirror. She'd have to make it a powerful one, though. It wouldn't help Ember if it knocked Issy out and left her cousin to fight Len on her own. "You always were smart in school, got the best grades, and now you're the right-hand man to the wealthiest family in Silver Hollow. Seems you were always destined for great things, Len."

"I am pretty smart, not going to lie." Len gave a smug chuckle, and Issy swallowed hard against the bile rising in her throat. Lying had never sat well with her, and lying to a known killer didn't make the situation any better. Still, she would do what had to be done to save Ember and herself. "How'd you get the staff at the Tropic Ranch Hotel to keep quiet about you and Troy staying there?" Issy asked. "Surely someone on the staff or one of the other guests might've mentioned you and Troy being there, especially after your hasty departure."

"Pffttt." Len grinned. "That part was easy. The staff I paid off. The other guests were mostly drunk and unreliable witnesses, so no need for money. They discredited themselves. Even poor Scott Brundage was easy enough to fool. The guy was so wasted he blacked out most of the trip. Then, as soon as the news broke of Sarah's murder, Troy's dad pulled some strings to avoid any bad publicity from our ill-advised trip and any association between the body and the Holland family name." Len gave a disgusted sigh. "Old Mr. Holland was always so worried about a scandal. He never did ask either of us about our involvement with Sarah Landers. Probably didn't want to know, in case he heard something he didn't like. Like I said, once we were back home in Silver Hollow, Troy and I worked on the internship program the rest of the week to support our alibi. We even made up elaborate scenarios to vouch for each other during the time we'd missed down in Florida. We were each other's alibi. And, of course, Troy's dad has pull."

Issy thought back to their meeting with Gladys and how the older lady had mentioned the elder Mr. Holland not wanting his name linked to any scandal. She sidled closer to Len, taking a deep breath and clenching her fists, preparing her magic to strike. "Why don't you let my cousin go, Len? Like she said, we won't say a word to anyone."

As if realizing just how close Issy had gotten, Len frowned and tightened his hold on Ember again. "Stay back!" he yelled, pressing the gun harder against Ember's temple. "What are you girls playing at?"

"Nothing." Issy squinted as headlights glared in brightly through the living room windows.

Len inhaled sharply and scowled at Issy, his tone accusatory. "You brought the cops!"

"No." Issy held her position though her knees were knocking. "I swear, we didn't. Please don't hurt Ember."

"Shut up!" Len looked around wildly, as if searching for an escape route. "There's no more time for talking. I need to get out of here."

Through the brilliant white light now filling the room, Issy saw Len's hands shaking, his finger trembling on the trigger of the gun. If he made one slip, one false move, he could kill her cousin, possibly kill her too...

Without another thought for her own safety, Issy unclenched her tight fists and hurled the first nonharmful spell she could think of at Len—a fainting spell. Unfortunately, with all the tension in the air and her own hands shaking from fear and adrenaline, Issy's aim was off.

The spell hit Ember instead, and she sagged heavily against Len, dead weight in his arms.

Unable to support Ember and still hold the gun, Len dropped her to the floor and aimed directly for Issy instead.

"Say hi to Sarah for me," Len said, his icy tone chilling.

Time seemed to slow around Issy as she watched Len pull the trigger. More headlights beamed into the windows, spotlighting the scene as she threw herself to the ground, instinctively trying to avoid the bullet. Sirens wailed and tires screeched on the asphalt driveway. Through a haze of smoke and the acrid stench of gunpowder, Issy crawled across the debris-riddled floor toward her cousin. "Ember? Are you okay?"

Behind her, she was vaguely aware of a loud crash. With her cousin cradled in her arm, she turned to see the front door kicked open and Dex standing there like an avenging angel.

"Come here!" Before Issy could resist, Len grabbed her around the neck, like he had Ember, and yanked her to her feet. The only difference this time was that Dex had his weapon pulled as well, pointing it at Len.

And he looked more than ready to use it, if his harsh expression was any indication.

Chapter Twenty-Six

In a split second, Dex took in the scene before him. Ember on the floor, unmoving. No visible blood, so she could be unconscious. Issy held captive, sheer terror in her eyes. Dex's gut clenched tight. Len Childs sneering behind her, the barrel of his semiautomatic aimed straight for Dex's heart.

His first instinct was to shoot first and ask questions later.

Except that Len held Issy before him like a shield. No way Dex could take the shot and not hit her. And he'd rather shoot himself than hit Issy with a bullet. As if sensing this, Len grinned and slowly moved the gun until it rested against the side of Issy's soft neck, right over her jugular. Issy's gorgeous green eyes widened as she stared at Dex, a silent plea in her gaze. She was paranormal, made of magic, yet she seemed completely helpless. He wasn't sure why, but the idea gutted him just the same.

Looked like it would be up to him this time to save the day.

"Put the gun down, Mr. Childs, and let's discuss this," Dex said, narrowing his gaze on Issy. He willed her to stay calm even as his own pulse thundered loudly in his ears. "You don't want to do this. There are other cops right behind me, and you can't get away."

"Shut up!" Len shouted. "You drop *your* gun, or I'll shoot your pretty little girlfriend here."

Can't. Fail. This. Time.

Dex kept repeating that mantra in his head even as flashes of the old kidnapping case flooded his mind. This time would be different. This time he would save the day because this time there was even more at stake, at least where his heart was concerned. This time Issy's life rested in his hands, and he wouldn't, couldn't let her down.

He needed a plan, something clever to get her away from Len. He tried stepping closer, but with each footstep, Len's hold around Issy's neck tightened. Issy gasped for breath, clawing at Len's forearm until Dex was scared she'd suffocate.

"Drop the weapon," Len repeated, shoving his gun harder into the side of Issy's neck. "Do it, or I'll shoot her. I swear I will. Blow her head off and get out of here before you even take another step at me."

Running through all his training in his head, Dex knew the key to apprehending Len was to get the guy to relax. The second his gun slipped away from Issy's neck, Dex would strike. Now, how to accomplish that? It had been a long time since those classes at Quantico, and Dex hadn't thought he'd need those tactics anymore after moving to the paranormal division. But he'd been wrong. He glanced over and caught Issy's eye again, saw the fear in their seafoam-green depths but also saw a spark of her affection for him there. And in that instant he knew. What he and Issy had was right.

Never mind that she rushed into danger. Never mind that she was some kind of witch. Dex had been wrong about a lot of things when he'd first come to Silver Hollow. Dex didn't plan on being wrong about things anymore.

"You're right, Len." Dex stepped closer and crouched, as if he was going to put his gun on the floor. His gaze never left Len's finger, trembling on the trigger of his weapon. "I can't win. I can't let you shoot Issy, so I'm putting my gun down."

Len's stiff posture visibly relaxed, and the barrel of his weapon veered slightly away from Issy's neck, pointing toward the ceiling instead. Seizing his opportunity, Dex lunged for Len, knocking the gun from Len's hand and sending it flying across the living room. Both men tumbled to the floor, allowing Issy to scramble away to relative safety beside her still-comatose cousin.

Dex wrestled with Len, throwing punches when he could and attempting to trap his opponent's hands behind his back so he could restrain him. Len was stronger than he looked, however, and managed to squirm out from beneath Dex and make a run for the open front door.

"Get him!" Issy yelled to Dex.

Adrenaline and determination buzzing through his system, Dex jumped to his feet and headed to block Len's escape. Len turned quickly and veered toward the kitchen instead, most likely hoping to escape through the breezeway. Dex was faster, though, and tackled him to the tile floor, this time managing to get a set of cuffs on the guy.

Standing, but keeping a foot on Len's back to prevent him from running again, Dex stared out into the murky half-light of the living room and spotted Issy helping her cousin to sit up. Apparently sometime during the scuffle Ember had awakened. Ember frowned at Issy then glanced over at Dex. "You just saved my life. Issy's too. Which means you guys are even. Not bonded anymore."

Bonded? What the heck did that mean? He shot Issy a confused look.

Issy gave him a reassuring smile. "Never mind Ember. I think she's got a concussion."

"There is nothing wrong with my head," Ember said, frowning at Issy. "I'm just pointing out—"

Len bucked beneath Dex's foot, and he scowled down darkly at his prisoner to quell any signs of rebellion. Len Childs was going to jail, then to trial, and Dex fully intended to see justice served. He pulled out his phone and hit the speed dial number for Owen, holding the phone to his ear with his shoulder as he peered out at Issy once more.

Ember might be a bit kooky sometimes, but Dex understood what she was saying. Issy had saved his life that night at Enid Pettywood's, using her magical skills to protect him. By doing so, she'd made Dex feel unworthy, made him feel like a failure for not defending those under his care. For the second time in his life, he'd screwed up—first the kidnapping case, then Issy. Tonight, he'd redeemed himself. Tonight, they'd become equals again.

"Where are you?" Owen said, his voice terse as he answered Dex's call.

"Jerry Blaisdale's kitchen. I've got Len Childs in custody and need backup to bring him in."

"I'm en route and should be there along with DeeDee in five minutes." Owen ended the call before

Dex could say more, and he couldn't help but chuckle as he shoved the phone back in his pocket. Issy and Ember hugged in the living room. Issy's smile lit up Dex's entire world, and the double-edged sword of love and regret pierced his heart. It was then that he knew.

Issy wasn't hurt, she'd done a good job of staving off Len and keeping him from shooting her or Ember. He knew that Issy was mysterious and magical and would always rush into danger. And he also knew he couldn't always be there to protect her.

It was then that Dex made his final decision on the lease for the bungalow.

Chapter Twenty-Seven

Two days later...

"Have I mentioned lately how nice it is to sit outside and not have to fend off a flurry of toads?" DeeDee said, taking a seat at what had become the Quinns' regular table outside The Main Squeeze.

"It's wonderful that we are having this unusual warm spell," Raine said. She'd foregone juice completely in favor of a plain bottled water. "It's brought a lot of townies out."

The outdoor tables were more crowded than usual. People stood in line for pizza. Issy squinted at the front of the line, where a charcoal-gray cat sat just under the pizza counter. He turned one golden-orange eye toward her and winked then flicked his mouth up to catch an anchovy Luigi flipped from the counter. Leave it to Brimstone to get a handout at a pizza joint.

"We were just discussing Len's arraignment hearing yesterday." Issy turned her attention back to their table and took a sip of her Pomegranate Passion. "Poor Troy sat there through the whole thing, looking completely mortified. I guess he really didn't have any idea Len had anything to do with Sarah Landers's murder."

"Yeah." DeeDee took a drink of her Sunrise Special. "I talked to him outside the courthouse after the hearing, and he said he was horrified. More so that his father's plan to help them avoid the limelight and scandal for the family name had inadvertently created an alibi for Len to get away with the killing of that girl."

"Then there's poor Scott Brundage," Raine said. "He got blamed for what happened down in Florida, and his whole life was ruined."

"At least Troy tried to help him out," Ember said. Her new Green Goddess Smoothie sat untouched on the table as she snuggled her familiars in her arms. "He gave Scott money for all those years to make sure he had food and clothes, not to keep him hooked on drugs like we thought."

"I heard this morning Troy Holland is starting a new charity in town devoted to feeding the homeless of Silver Hollow," Gray said. "Guess he's one of the good guys after all."

"Yep," Issy agreed, holding her hand up over her eyes to block out the bright midday sun. "Jerry Blaisdale? Is that you?" She waved the town mechanic over. "How was your vacation?"

"Good, really good," Jerry said, stopping by their table on the way into the juice bar. "Man, what a mess to come back to, though, eh?" Jerry shook his head and frowned. "I feel bad I didn't know Troy and Len were lying about the internship program that summer."

"They fooled us all," Issy said.

"Yeah. They fooled me twice, though." Jerry shook his head. "Len gave me that bogus free vacation back then too, said I'd won some contest at the paper mill. It worked. Kept me out of town during Scott's trial so I couldn't repudiate what they'd said in their testimony. I never even knew about it."

"I'm surprised no one questioned you about that program back then," Raine said.

Jerry shrugged. "Well, I was just a security guard, so no one asked me anything. Especially after the internship program supervisor verified Len and Troy were there the whole time. No need to ask any more questions after that, right?"

"What about Linda saying you wanted to be a PI?" Gray asked. "Was that true?"

"Oh yeah." Jerry smiled. "I've always loved a good mystery, so when Linda Brewer contacted me to help her investigate the murder, of course I said yes. I tried to get Adele to tell me about Scott's state of mind back then, and that's why she and I argued during the wake.

I felt bad, though, and went outside to cool off, and that's when Marcy talked to me. Poor thing was so distraught over losing Scott and the fact Adele wouldn't give her anything to remember the man she loved by, that I told her I had an old camera from back in the day that might have pictures of Scott on it." Jerry wrinkled his nose and looked away. "Of course, Len couldn't have those pictures getting out, so he sent me on another free vacation before I was able to retrieve the camera from storage." Sadness fell over his expression, and his right shoulder twitched, sending the drinks on the next table tumbling to the ground. "Len's right. I am stupid."

"No, Jerry. You're not stupid at all." Issy exchanged a look with her cousins. "You're kindhearted and see the good in people. That's not stupid. That's brave."

"Yeah?" he said, not meeting Issy's gaze.

"Yeah." She smiled. "Now go get your juice and some lunch."

Jerry's spirits seemed to lift a bit, and he squared his shoulders. "Thanks, Quinns. All of your next oil changes are on me, okay? You too, Deputy."

"Okay." The cousins grinned and waved as Jerry headed inside the shop.

"Thanks, Jer," DeeDee called then took another huge gulp of her drink while she checked her cell phone. "Yes! Owen just texted me. He tracked down the garbage truck that emptied the dumpster at Holland Mills that day before it went to the incinerator. He dug through the trash and located Adele's appointment book and several missing photo albums, even found some from when Scott was a baby. Basically, all of the ones Len confessed to stealing that night he killed Adele." DeeDee switched off her phone and sat back in her chair. "Since Len didn't know which albums had which pictures, he just grabbed them all and ran. Owen said he even found some more photos of the Tropic Ranch Hotel mixed in."

"Speaking of Owen," Issy said, pausing to kiss Bella's cute little head. "Isn't he supposed to join us here today?"

DeeDee snorted. "I wouldn't expect him anytime soon. Poor guy said he's on his tenth shower, trying to wash off the stink of all that garbage he had to dig through."

"Ew." Ember scrunched her nose and sipped her drink while surveying the bustling sidewalks of Silver Hollow. "And that's exactly why I could never be a police officer."

"Among other reasons." Gray winked then glanced past DeeDee and grinned. "Um, don't look now, Deputy, but I think someone has the hots for you."

"Huh?" DeeDee pulled a face and swiveled. "Oh no."

Issy glanced across the town green to see Caine Hunter, the hotshot movie producer, giving DeeDee an appraising head-to-toe stare. Issy didn't miss the way her favorite female wolf shifter turned away fast or the telltale blush that stained her cheeks. Seemed DeeDee might be more interested in their new Hollywood big shot than she was letting on.

"He is *so* not the type of man I go for," DeeDee said, toying with her nearly empty cup.

She protested a bit too much in Issy's opinion. Caine was good looking, even Issy could admit that. And quite wealthy. Good with the ladies too, if the rumors were true. Not exactly the kind of man most women would kick to the curb. Doing her best to keep her tone neutral, Issy asked, "Why don't you like him?"

"He's too full of himself. Always strutting around like he's a gift to the female population." DeeDee rolled her eyes. "Who needs to deal with a man who's prettier than you?"

The girls laughed, and Gray just shook his head.

"Besides," DeeDee continued, "my oat-sowing days are almost over." She gave a side-glance toward the sexy producer once more then frowned. "I don't know. Maybe one last fling wouldn't be such a bad idea. Not with him, though. I've been called out to the mansion where he's staying once already on police business, and I have to say that I'm not impressed. I don't like his style. Too showy and over the top."

"Hey, Quinns!" Dex strolled up to their table with Gordon perched on his shoulder. "What are you all doing out and about this fine autumn day?"

"Hello, Dex." DeeDee pushed to her feet and gave Issy a wink. "I was just leaving. Please, take my seat."

"Oh, okay. Thanks." He settled in beside Issy, and the tiny bearded dragon on his shoulder raised his front paw to her as if in greeting. She couldn't resist reaching over and shaking the little lizard's hand. Okay, so maybe he wasn't quite so little anymore. In fact, he'd grown large enough he barely fit on Dex's shoulder anymore. Still, he'd always be a baby to her.

Dex! Dex is here, Mommy! We like Dex, Mommy! We love Dex!

Bella pranced and panted on Issy's lap, overjoyed to see her favorite FBPI agent again.

Issy did her best not to get flustered when Dex reached under the table and took her hand.

"Well." Ember tucked her felines back into their basket before picking up her Green Goddess cup from the table. "I hate to drink and run, but I really need to go back to my shop. Busy day." She elbowed Raine in the shoulder and gave her a pointed smile. "Don't you have things to do as well?"

"No." Raine frowned up as Ember poked her again. "Ow! Okay, fine." She pushed to her feet and straightened the black cardigan she'd thrown on to cover her usual overalls and T-shirt. "Despite you two not being soul-bonded anymore, my money's still on you getting together."

Heat prickled Issy's cheeks, and she hazarded a glance at Dex to check his response. If he had any, he didn't show it, thankfully. "Right," she said to her cousins. "Have a good afternoon."

"You too." Ember tugged Raine away by the arm. "Don't do anything I wouldn't."

Gray chuckled and slapped Dex on the back then tossed his trash into the bin behind him and stood. "See you both later."

"Be right back." Dex headed into the juice bar, returning moments later with his own Pomegranate Passion.

"So," Issy said once she and Dex were alone and settled again. She looked everywhere but him, stroking her fingers through Bella's soft fur as the little dog stared up at Dex like he was a god on earth. As much as Issy wanted to be with Dex, he was leaving. He'd all but told her he was trying to get out of his lease when she'd been at his bungalow. Long-distance relationships never worked out, especially when the two people involved were so different. He might have accepted her magical abilities, yes, but that didn't mean he wanted to live with them day in and day out.

Dex! Dex! Dex! We love Dex, Mommy! We love Dex!

"So." Dex swallowed a large gulp of his juice before turning to face her, his hazel eyes warm with affection. "Nice day out, huh?"

"Yeah. I hear the temperatures are supposed to rise steadily by this weekend." Small talk was the last thing she wanted to partake in, but words seemed beyond her at this point. "The colors are amazing now too."

"Yep, gorgeous." He nodded, his gaze never leaving hers as he took another sip of his juice then fed Gordon a slice of orange from his cup. "Listen, Issy..."

"Yes?" Her voice had gone all breathy without her consent.

Bella squirmed on her lap.

We love Dex, Mommy! We love Dex!

"I was wondering..." His dark brows drew together, and he cleared his throat, resting his forearms on the table. "Well, I was wondering if maybe you weren't busy tonight, if you would possibly want to go out to dinner with me again? We could try that little French bistro once more or anyplace, really. I'd just really like to see you again."

Issy's heart skipped a crazy beat. This was what she'd wanted, what she'd hoped for and dreamed about for so long, but now that the moment was here, she was scared. Scared of how badly she wanted things to work out with Dex and how shattered she'd be if they didn't.

She took a deep breath and narrowed her gaze, forcing the words out. "I'm not sure that's such a good idea."

"Why not?" Dex looked over at her, his frown darkening. "I thought you liked me, Issy. Lord knows I like you, way more than I ever expected."

"I do like you, Dex. So much. It's just that we're so different, and I understand getting involved with a witch isn't something most mortal men want to do. Maybe we should just leave things as they are and save both of us some heartache." She blinked back the unexpected sting of tears and kissed Bella's head again. "After all, you're leaving town soon anyway, and I'm sure you'll have no problem finding a normal girl who'll love you."

Don't cry, Mommy! Dex is here! We love Dex! Dex loves us too!

"Leaving?" Dex straightened, scowling. "Who told you that?"

"You did." Issy narrowed her gaze. "The other day at your bungalow you said you wanted to break your lease."

He gave a short laugh and looked up into the clear blue sky. "Lord save me from assuming witches." Then he looked at Issy again, the gold flecks in his hazel eyes sparkling with heat. "I said I wanted to *get out* of the lease. Not break it. I want out so I can *buy* the bungalow. You can't get rid of me that easy."

"Oh," Issy said absently, too wrapped up in the tingles zinging through her bloodstream from his caress. When his statement finally penetrated her love-dazed brain, her eyes snapped to his. "Wait. You're staying?"

"That's what I said." He grinned and reached over to slide a strawberry-blond curl behind her ear, his touch lingering on her cheek. "If you don't mind, I'd like to stick around and discover everything magical about you." His gaze flickered to her lips before returning to her eyes. He stood and held out his hand. "Besides, I need some help decorating my new place. I hoped maybe you could swing by and help me figure out where to put this new chair I bought."

"Sure." Issy placed Bella on the ground then took Dex's hand and pushed to her feet. Her heart was racing, and she felt more alive than she could ever remember. All because of this man—this man she'd never expected to find but couldn't imagine living without. "I'd be delighted."

Bella pranced at her side and Gordon waved to passersby as she and Dex headed toward his Buick parked along the curb.

Dex! Dex! Dex! We love Dex, Mommy! We love Dex!

Yes we do, Issy sent back to her little Pom telepathically. *Yes we do.*

Just as they reached Dex's vehicle, his cell phone buzzed. He pulled it out of his pocket and checked the screen as he held the door for Issy and Bella. "Darn it."

"What's wrong?" Issy asked as she got into the Buick then settled the tiny dog on her lap.

Dex shut her door then jogged around the front of his car to climb behind the wheel. "It's Stan, my old partner. Remember him?"

Issy remembered. She suppressed a shudder as she fastened her seat belt. "Yes. Why?"

"Well, he's all worked up about that new movie producer in town." Dex started the engine. "He swears that new film of his is full of real vampires and werewolves. In fact, he's coming to town next week to check it out."

Taking a deep breath, Issy waited until they'd signaled and pulled out into traffic before leaning over and kissing Dex on the cheek. "Don't worry. With what I know about paranormals and your knowledge of the FBPI, I think we can handle Stan." Issy kissed Dex again just because it felt so darned good then squeezed his free hand in hers. "Right now we have a bungalow to decorate."

About Leighann Dobbs

USA Today Bestselling author Leighann Dobbs has had a passion for reading since she was old enough to hold a book, but she didn't put pen to paper until much later in life. After a twenty-year career as a software engineer with a few side trips into selling antiques and making jewelry, she realized you can't make a living reading books, so she tried her hand at writing them and discovered she had a passion for that, too! She lives in New Hampshire with her husband, Bruce, their trusty Chihuahua mix, Mojo, and beautiful rescue cat, Kitty.

Find out about her latest books and how to get discounts on them by signing up at:

http://www.leighanndobbs.com/newsletter

If you want to receive a text message alert on your cell phone for new releases, text COZYMYSTERY to 88202 (sorry, this only works for US cell phones!)

Connect with Leighann on Facebook:

https://www.facebook.com/leighanndobbs books

Also By Leighann Dobbs

COZY MYSTERIES

Silver Hollow

Paranormal Cozy Mystery Series

* * *

A Spell of Trouble

Spell Disaster

Blackmoore Sisters

Cozy Mystery Series

* * *

Dead Wrong

Dead & Buried

Dead Tide

Buried Secrets

Deadly Intentions

A Grave Mistake

Spell Found

Mooseamuck Island

Cozy Mystery Series

* * *

A Zen For Murder

A Crabby Killer

A Treacherous Treasure

Mystic Notch

Cat Cozy Mystery Series

* * *

Ghostly Paws

A Spirited Tail

A Mew To A Kill

Paws and Effect

Lexy Baker

Cozy Mystery Series

* * *

Lexy Baker Cozy Mystery Series Boxed Set Vol 1

(Books 1-4)

Or buy the books separately:

Killer Cupcakes

Dying For Danish

Murder, Money and Marzipan

3 Bodies and a Biscotti

Brownies, Bodies & Bad Guys

Bake, Battle & Roll

Wedded Blintz

Scones, Skulls & Scams

Ice Cream Murder

Mummified Meringues

Brutal Brulee (Novella)

No Scone Unturned

———

Witches of Hawthorne Grove Series:

Something Magical (Book 1)

———

Regency Romance

***

The Unexpected Series:

An Unexpected Proposal

Dobbs Fancytales:

Dobbs Fancytales Boxed Set Collection

_____

Western Historical Romance

***

Goldwater Creek Mail Order Brides:

Faith

American Mail Order Brides Series:

Chevonne: Bride of Oklahoma

____

Contemporary Romance

***

Reluctant Romance

———

281

Sweetrock Cowboy Romance Series:
Some Like It Hot (Book 1)
Too Close For Comfort (Book 2)

———